Loving You Is A Battle 3

Tina J

Copyright 2019

This novel is a work of fiction. Any resemblances to actual events, real people, living or dead, organizations, establishments or locales are products of the author's imagination. Other names, characters, places, and incidents are used fictionally.

All parts reserved. No part of this book may be used or reproduced in any form or by any means electronic or mechanical, including photocopying, recording or by information storage and retrieval system, without written permission from the publisher and write.

Because of the dynamic nature of the Internet, any web address or links contained in this book may have changed since publication, and may no longer be valid.

Warning:

This book is strictly Urban Fiction and the story is **NOT**

REAL!

Characters will not behave the way you want them to; nor will they react to situations the way you think they should. Some of them may be drug addicts, kingpins, savages, thugs, rich, poor, ho's, sluts, haters, bitter ex-girlfriends or boyfriends, people from the past and the list can go on and on. That is what Urban Fiction mostly consists of. If this isn't anything you foresee yourself interested in, then do yourself a favor and don't read it because it's only going to piss you off. ☺☺

Also, the book will not end the way you want so please be advised that the outcome will be based solely on my own thoughts and ideas. I hope you enjoy this book that y'all made me write. Thanks so much to my readers, supporters, publisher and fellow authors and authoress for the support. ☺☺

Author Tina J

More books from me:

The Thug I Chose 1, 2 & 3

A Thin Line Between Me and My Thug 1 & 2

I Got Luv For My Shawty 1 & 2

Kharis and Caleb: A Different Kind of Love 1 & 2

Loving You Is A Battle 1 & 2 & 3

Violet and The Connect 1 & 2 & 3

You Complete Me

Love Will Lead You Back

This Thing Called Love

Are We In This Together 1,2 &3

Shawty Down To Ride For a Boss 1, 2 &3

When A Boss Falls in Love 1, 2 & 3

Let Me Be The One 1 & 2

We Got That Forever Love

Aint No Savage Like The One I Got 1&2

A Queen and A Hustla 1, 2 & 3

Thirsty For A Bad Boy 1&2

Hassan and Serena: An Unforgettable Love 1&2

Caught Up Loving A Beast 1, 2 & 3

A Street King And His Shawty 1 & 2

I Fell For The Wrong Bad Boy 1&2

I Wanna Love You 1 & 2

Addicted to Loving a Boss 1, 2, & 3

I Need That Gangsta Love 1&2

Creepin With The Plug 1 & 2

All Eyes On The Crown 1,2&3

When She's Bad, I'm Badder: Jiao and Dreek, A Crazy

Love Story 1,2&3

Still Luvin A Beast 1&2

Her Man, His Savage 1 & 2

Marco & Rakia: Not Your Ordinary, Hood Kinda Love 1,2

& 3

Feenin For A Real One 1, 2 & 3

A Kingpin's Dynasty 1, 2 & 3

What Kinda Love Is This: Captivating A Boss 1, 2 & 3

Frankie & Lexi: Luvin A Young Beast 1, 2 & 3

A Dope Boys Seduction 1, 2 & 3

My Brother's Keeper 1. 2 & 3

C'Yani & Meek: A Dangerous Hood Love 1, 2 & 3

When A Savage Falls for A Good Girl 1, 2 & 3

Eva & Deray 1 & 2

Blame It On His Gangsta Luv 1 & 2

Falling for The Wrong Hustla 1, 2 & 3

I Gave My Heart to A Jersey Killa 1, 2 & 3

Luvin The Son of a Savage 1, 2 & 3

A Dopeman and His Shawty 1, 2 & 3

Iesha

Four months had gone by and we still had no luck finding my sister. Hell, she didn't even contact me. My kids miss seeing her and their cousins just like I do.

I've been trying to keep myself busy to distract myself and it works until Cream shows up. He is a complete mess and in total denial that she would leave him and I agree. She was ecstatic to be marrying him and after she performed for him at his bachelor party and they had sex, there's no way she left. There was some foul play involved and the sooner we found out the better.

Cream has been staying with us since Ci Ci's been gone and that's fine because the kids love spending time with their uncle. He loves playing with them, but you can tell he misses his kids too. He and I have gone back to the spot her car was found thinking we'll find something, but we never do.

"Hey sis. What's for dinner?" He kissed my cheek and

sat at the table.

"I was in the mood for seafood so we're having shrimp scampi, but I made some lobster tails too. There's a salad in the fridge and baked potatoes in the oven."

"Damn that sounds good." Darius said walking in. He pecked me on the lips and sat down with us. We tried not to show too much affection in front of him. We didn't want to rub it in his face. Creams phone rang so Darius and I kept talking.

"Hello. Yo who the fuck is this?" He yelled in the phone. He said hello a few more times and hung up.

"What's up bro?" Darius turned to him.

"Nothing. I've been getting these phone calls lately where the person doesn't say shit. But keeps calling back."

"Then get the number changed." I thought he was going to kill Darius just off the way he looked at him.

"Are you crazy? What if Ci Ci tries to reach me?"

"A'ight man damn. She has our number too." Darius put his hands up.

"My bad man. I'm just stressed the fuck out. I'm going to take a plate and lay down. Tell the kids I'll play with them

8

tomorrow." We heard him shut the door.

"Baby maybe we should get your mom over here to talk to him."

"Why you say that?"

"Darius that is a broken man. He knows his wife wouldn't just leave him but he has no way to find her. She just disappeared without a trace and that shit just don't happen to black people."

"Black people? Really Iesha?"

"I'm serious. You see that shit on the news about white people all the time. You think I'm crazy but Ci Ci didn't leave him and I think someone has her I just don't know who."

"What about those bitches from the mall?" He asked me.

"I doubt those two idiots even know how to kidnap a mouse. Whoever did this, planned it and were waiting for the right time. The question now is who would want to make sure she left him for good? Who benefitted from it?"

Darius and I fed the kids and bathed them. They wanted to watch Kung Fu Panda as a family. I sent Summer and Lyric to knock on Cream's door since they were the oldest.

"Uncle Cream can you watch this movie with us?" He came out giving us the evil eye. We knew he wouldn't tell the kids no that's why we sent them. He needed to come out the room for some fresh air anyway. His phone rang again, and he went to answer it.

"This is the same number. Just listen." The kids weren't paying us any mind.

"Hello." He put it on speaker. You could hear something rattling in the background.

"That's J.J." Summer said lying on her stomach watching TV. We all looked at her like she was crazy as the person was still on the phone. She called James Jr. J.J. when I had my son because she said it was too many juniors.

"Summer come here honey." Cream called to her. She rolled over and got up slowly because she was into the movie.

"Baby how do you know that's JJ?"

"That's Pokémon music in the background. That's his favorite show playing on the background. You don't hear it?" He said he heard noise a few times but never paid attention to

10

the music.

"James Jr is that you?" The phone went dead. He gave Summer a big hug and went to get dressed. He came out and his phone rang again.

"Hello."

"Daddy." I saw the tears coming down Creams face.

"Junior, where are you?"

"Daddy, mommy's not waking up."

"Junior what's wrong with mommy?" Cream was pacing back and forth in the kitchen. We stepped out the living room so the kids wouldn't hear and get upset.

"She has red stuff coming out her ears and nose."

"Junior put the phone to mommy's ear."

"Daddy, I don't have a phone. I have an iPad." How was he calling me with an iPad? I would figure that out later.

"Ok son. Put the iPad to her ear." You could hear rustling in the background.

"Ci Ci baby, it's your husband. Baby, I need you to listen to my voice and tell me where you are." I was crying so hard, Darius had to hug me to keep me calm.

"Ci Ci please. I need you to find your strength to just tell me where you are?"

"James." I heard just above a whisper.

"Yes baby. I'm coming to get you; where are you?"

"James come get the kids."

"Ok baby. I need you to tell me where you are."

"James, I lost the baby." I gasped and covered my mouth. The look on his face was scary.

"What baby? Never mind. We can talk about that later. One more time baby, where are you?"

"Home."

"Home." We all said at the same time.

"Daddy, mommy went to sleep. When are you coming to get us? Grandma keeps hitting mommy and the monster man doesn't like to hear my sister cry."

All our mouths hung to the ground.

Tasha Barnes

As I look down at my daughter CiCi slowly dying, I couldn't do anything but feel sorry for what I've been doing to her; then I thought about how she wanted me to die.

The day we kidnapped her, I didn't plan on beating her the way I did. But since I couldn't get to Iesha I had to take all my frustrations and anger out on her. Sure, I could've stopped after the first time but every time I looked at CiCi all I saw was Iesha. I hated that child with a passion and it was my own fault. I told everyone I mistreated her because I was jealous of her and my husband's relationship but that was far from the truth. I hated her because she was the product of his infidelity.

When I first got with their father he was the man of my dreams and no one could tell me different. He treated me like a queen and gave me anything I wanted including my daughter CiCi. A few months after we had her he wanted to try for another child. Unfortunately; I suffered a miscarriage that made me hemorrhage so much I had to get a hysterectomy.

13

Therefore, not allowing me to birth any more kids. We were devastated and I fell into a state of depression. I wouldn't have sex with him; I started drinking heavy and didn't even care for my own daughter. It took months for me to get back to my old self.

One day when CiCi was two years old she and I were coming from the park; when we walked in the house and found my husband holding a newborn baby. I put my daughter down for a nap and went into the living room to speak with my husband about the child he was holding.

"Sit down Tasha. We need to talk." I knew right then something wasn't right.

"Whose baby is this?" He went on tell me when I slipped into depression he found comfort in another and the result ended up with him having another child.

"So not only did you cheat but you had a baby on me?"

"I'm sorry Tasha but it was time for me to tell you."

"Oh, now it's time. Don't you think the time should've come when you started sleeping around?" I started punching

and slapping him, not caring that he still had the baby in his hands.

"Tasha, calm down." He pushed me back so he could put the baby in her car seat. I continued fighting him until he pushed me against the wall and had my hands over my head.

"How could you?" The tears flowed swiftly down my face. He began to place kisses on my lips. Needless to say he took care of my body the way he usually did but it still didn't excuse him having a baby on me. The next few years I helped him raise her but I couldn't find it in my heart to love her like my own so I started doing mean shit to her over the years; like leaving her at school late or putting her in the oven and say she climbed in on her own.

The little bitch just wouldn't go away and throughout the years my hatred for her became worse; especially the way he spoiled her. I couldn't stand to look my husband in his eyes anymore and started poisoning him and had my lover who was a doctor tell him he had cancer. He believed it and when he took his last breath I couldn't be happier. Now if I can get to Iesha and do the same to her everything will be perfect.

"What are you in here thinking about?" Monster asked me as he poured me another shot of Jack.

"Oh nothing. Where the hell have you been?"

"Yo, I don't have to tell you shit."

"Who are you talking to? Remember all I have to make is a call and I have that two million dollars."

"Go ahead and make the call. I bet you won't get far when they find out its you."

"What do you mean by that?"

"It's just a matter of time before that nigga finds his wife and when he figures out it was you he's not going to have any mercy on you."

"I'm not worried about that. Shit, if my own daughter can't figure out who I am I know he won't either." I saw the look of shock on his face when I said that.

"Hold the fuck up yo. What do you mean if your daughter can't tell who you are?" I got up and walked over to where he was standing and kissed on his neck. I could tell he was getting aroused by the way his dick tried coming out his pants.

16

"That's right. Ci Ci is my daughter." He pushed me so hard it felt like the wind was knocked out of me as I hit the wall. I got up laughing and sat back at the table.

"You have to be kidding me. Don't tell me I've been fucking my girl's mom."

"Sorry to say you have been." I continued laughing pissing him off more. I wasn't going to tell him Iesha wasn't really my daughter. I was getting a kick out of watching him sweat.

"But how. I know her mom and you're not her." He was pacing back and forth.

"After that nigga Darius almost killed me in the hospital I was in a coma. When I woke up I was handcuffed to the bed with around the clock officers outside my door. So imagine my surprise when a detective Williams came in offering me a deal."

"What type of deal did my sister offer you?"

"I forgot that was your sister. Well, she told me she had a friend who specialized in plastic surgery and if I did something for her she would return the favor."

"What was the favor?" He asked staring down at me.

"Who knew she was obsessed over my daughters husband? The same nigga that tried to break my arm and keep me away from my grandson."

"What was the fucking deal?" He yelled trying to figure out what his sister and I did.

"It was really easy if you ask me. All she wanted was for me to tell her what his weakness was and to give her an idea on how to get him to sleep with her. Your sister was crazy though. She wanted to have his kids and had this idea about killing CiCi and having him all to herself. She was going to kill her the day she pulled her over but CiCi hit her and pulled off."

"Wait. You were ok with her killing your own flesh and blood?"

"I don't give a fuck about CiCi anymore. The day Darius threw me out Iesha's room in the hospital and told everyone to let me die she did all this to herself."

"I can't believe this shit. What kind of mother does this to her kids?" He got up to leave but I jumped in front of him. I stripped down to my birthday suit and saw his dick grow again.

I dropped and took him in my mouth until he let all his babies slide down my throat. Thank goodness he was still hard because I needed to be fucked right then. He bent me over and had me screaming his name over and over.

After we were finished we laid on the dining room floor breathing heavy when I swore I heard a man's voice. I glanced over at him and he shrugged his shoulders. We both threw our clothes on and searched the house for the voice. Neither of us could figure out where it came from. We stopped at the room I held my daughter hostage in and heard my grandson telling his father how I keep beating his mom and that Monster doesn't like his sister crying. *FUCK!*

Monster

I came to the house to tell Tasha I was ready to send CiCi and her kids back to her man. I was over this kidnapping shit and that Iesha was my focus. When this bitch told me she was their mom I almost shit myself. I couldn't believe she was treating her daughter that way; better yet I couldn't believe I had fucked her.

I knew if Iesha found out she would never take me back. Then to find out her and my sister came up with a scheme to have her face changed and kill Cream's wife had me at a loss for words. I was getting ready to leave when she dropped and gave me some of her bomb head. This was going to be my last time so I may as well give her what she wanted.

When we heard a man's voice the both of us searched high and low for it. To hear Junior talking to his dad through the damn iPad let me know it was time to go. I looked down on the floor and CiCi had blood coming from her eyes and nose. I didn't want to say it but home girl looked dead to me. I could hear Cream yelling for Junior to keep talking.

"Junior has left the building." I said grabbing the Ipad and just to get under his skin.

"Monster, I swear on my life that I am coming for you and her mother."

"Aww man shut the fuck up. You're talking a lot of shit for someone who has no idea where they are." He laughed into the phone, which made me a little nervous. I've always heard that if he did that, it meant death to that person. I wasn't scared but I wasn't ready to leave this earth yet either.

"Yea nigga you thought I was dead but I'm alive and well. You will never find me. Oh and you can say goodbye to your precious CiCi because it looks like she checked out." The line went dead and the Ipad's screen lit up showing the apps on it.

"We have to get the fuck out of here." I told Tasha and she stood there staring at Junior and the baby. I saw her walking over to Junior but couldn't get to her in time and watched her punch Junior in the face so hard he fell on the ground banging his head. When CiCi didn't move or scream I knew for a fact she was dead.

"Yo, what the fuck is wrong with you? That's a motherfucking kid. I should beat your ass for that." I yanked her up before she hit the baby. I could care less about how much those kids cried for their dad I would never do any shit like that to them. I threw her in the basement and locked that shit.

We were supposed to do that to CiCi and the kids and tell Cream where they were after I got Iesha but she fucked that up. I heard a loud thump and went back in the room. When I got in there the baby was screaming her head off. She must've rolled off the bed and now her head had a gash in it. This shit was beyond crazy.

I ran to my car with Junior and the baby and put them in the back seat. Junior was still breathing but it seemed like his breaths were shallow. I grabbed CiCi and she felt like dead weight. I felt bad for her but like I told her a life for a life. My sister didn't deserve to die because she pulled her over. The way I looked at it was the nigga was lucky his kids were still alive.

I drove to the hospital and parked outside the emergency room but didn't go inside right away. The baby had finally cried herself to sleep. I went inside and found a wheelchair in the vestibule. I put CiCi in it and placed Junior on her lap. Her head was all the way back and Junior was sliding out the chair. I pushed the chair inside the ER, ran back to my car to get the baby and sat her next to them and bounced. I looked back and saw Junior on the ground and the baby was lying there crying. I sat in my car watching until I started seeing people running to the door where they were. I pulled off knowing I did my good deed for the day.

When I got back to the house I snatched Tasha's dumb ass out the basement and made her get all her stuff. She started talking shit like she always did and I shut the shit down by punching her in the fucking mouth. I think I knocked two of her teeth out. I didn't give a fuck either, that was for CiCi's son.

Cream

When I hung the phone up on Monster after he said that shit about me not knowing where he was with my family. I couldn't wait to open the door and beat his ass before I killed him.

Unfortunately, when we got to my house no one was there. We searched every room and came up with nothing. It didn't even look like anyone had been there since the last time I was there. I was at a loss because I didn't understand why my wife said she was home and that's not where she really was. I started pacing back and forth when my phone started ringing. I didn't recognize the number and decided to answer it just in case it was my son again.

"Hello."

"James is that you?" I heard the caller ask.

"Damien right now is not a good time."

"I know its not but you need to listen."

"Damien, just shut the club down if you can't handle it."

"James, listen. I'm at the hospital with my man and I just saw them bring CiCi and the kids in." I dropped the phone and ran out the house with everyone following behind me. I felt like my heart had been ripped out hearing that my family was at the hospital. That could only mean one thing and I was praying to God they were all ok. I had to be doing 90 the entire way. I didn't even care that I had two cop cars following behind me with their lights on. I pulled up in front of the ER and ran inside. I saw Damien crying and knew something wasn't right.

"Where are they?" He could barely speak which was pissing me off. I saw my brother talking to the cops outside as I waited for Damien to speak. Iesha walked in as he started talking.

"James, I was waiting for my man to get his discharge papers when I heard all this commotion. Now you know me being as nosy as I am I ran out." He paused like he was trying to find the words to speak.

"Damien what did you see?" Iesha asked him. He was now sitting in the chair. I had to sit myself just to keep from knocking him the fuck out. He was taking too long to tell me what he saw and the receptionist said I had to wait for a doctor to come out.

"Patience was on the ground crying with a gash on her forehead. Junior was lying there and if I didn't know any better I would say his nose was broken. There was blood all over his face and it was out of place."

"I know you're fucking with me right now Damien. There's no way anybody put their hands on my kids like that. I had him hemmed up against the wall. I could tell he was scared to tell me anything else but if he knows what's good for him he better.

"What about my wife?" Darius and Louis pulled me off of him.

"I'm sorry James. CiCi didn't look good. I grabbed her hand when they put her on the stretcher and tried to talk to her. Her hands were cold and she didn't wake up." It was as if everything stopped after he said that. I pulled my gun out my waist and pointed it at the security guard.

"Take me in the back right fucking now to my kids and my wife." He was so scared he peed on himself. As he was taking me to the back a nurse came out with my daughter who had a patch over her forehead and sucking on a bottle.

"Wait, right there. If you move I swear I'm killing you." I took my daughter from the nurse and kissed her all over her face. I hugged her tight until I heard her start crying. Iesha took her from me and the nurse started telling me what was going on with my son.

"Your son suffered what looks like a broken nose and a concussion. The doctors will know more after the x-ray. Whoever did it used so much force that had it been any harder, it probably would've killed him. I'm sorry this happened to your family sir and as soon as he's out of x-ray I will come to get you."

"Do you know what's going on with my wife?" I asked her hoping she knew the answer.

"I work in the pediatric department but if you give me a few minutes I can try and find out for you."

"Listen, I know this has nothing to do with any of you but if a doctor doesn't come out here and tell me something within the next five minutes I'm killing y'all one by one." She took off running to the back and I swear exactly four minutes later a doctor walked out.

"Hi, I'm doctor Watson and I am the one taking care of your wife. I understand what you are going through and I am here to answer a few questions for you quickly because I have to get back to her." He shook my hand and walked us over to a quiet area.

"Is she going to be ok? Is she alive?" I started asking him every question that came to my mind.

"Your wife was dropped off here almost an hour and a half ago and had the person waited another few hours she would be deceased. When she came in her heart rate was at a 20 and she was barely breathing. Her body was badly bruised and malnourished. We ran a cat scan and an MRI on her.

She has a collapsed lung, a few cracked ribs, three fingers on her right hand appear to be broken, one of her ankles is turned in the opposite direction. She had blood coming from her ears and when we checked; her right eardrum is busted, which may result in a loss of hearing on that side. Her nose isn't broken but it's swollen and one of her eyes is completely shut. She also has an extensive amount of swelling on the brain. We need your permission to operate on her right now or we're going to lose her."

I shook my head yes because no words would come out. I shook his hand and listened to my brother tell him to make sure he comes out as soon as the surgery was over. Louis apologized to the security guard for me and gave him a little something for what happened. I took Patience and laid her on my chest as I waited to hear about my son and wife.

A few hours later a pediatric doctor came out and told me I could go and see my son. The surgery wasn't needed after all but his nose was severely bruised and he had a concussion. He was awake and told the doctor and nurses what his grandmother did to him and his mom. When I walked in the back I saw the sad look on all their faces and as bad as I wanted to black out I didn't. I grabbed my son and squeezed him just as tight as I did my daughter.

"Daddy, what took you so long to find us?" My son asked sitting on my lap and playing with my phone like he always did.

"I'm sorry son. I didn't know where you guys were? Your grandmother kept you hidden very well." I said as Iesha took him from me and sat him on her lap.

"You know grandma had us staying at the house. You could've just come over." I gave him a crazy look because there were no signs of them at the house.

"Junior I went to the house and you weren't there."

"Not our big house daddy, the smaller one. You know when you and mommy were mad at each other we stayed in the smaller one." My son was smart as hell.

"I'll be right back Junior. Iesha can you and Maria stay in here with him and Patience?" When she shook her head yes I grabbed Louis and Darius and stepped outside.

"What's up?" Louis asked me lighting a black and mild.

"Do you know how many times I rode by that fucking house? I saw the lights on and assumed someone moved in there. I didn't even think to go there. My family was being fucking tortured right under my nose and I didn't even know it. What kind of father and husband am I? Who allows this to happen to their family?" I hit the wall outside so hard two of the bones came out my hand and blood was everywhere.

"Calm the fuck down Cream. There was no way you could've known they were there. Remember we all thought she left." Darius said trying to make sense of it.

"Nah. I knew she didn't leave me. I kept telling y'all she didn't. What the fuck man? Now my wife is fighting for her life; somebody put their hands on my fucking kids. I about to paint this town red." I walked back inside and the same doctor that told us about my wife's condition came out the back. You could tell he was looking for us because his head was looking everywhere but where we were standing.

"Mr. Thomas. I need you to follow me." He opened the door and we went behind him. He looked down at my hand and

31

sent me straight to the x-ray department. I was in and out within ten minutes.

"Mr. Thomas I'm going to give you and update about your wife but your hand is broken and you have two bones sticking out. You are going to need surgery right away."

"No disrespect doc but I'm not doing shit until I see my wife. My hand can fall off and I wouldn't care right now." I told him and he shook his head. He gave me a rundown of everything he told me prior.

"Mrs. Thomas is currently in the recovery room but she will be moved to ICU."

"What for? You said everything went well in surgery."

"Mr. Thomas your wife had a traumatic brain injury that caused intracranial pressure which was preventing blood from flowing to her brain; and was depriving her of oxygen. Your wife was slowly dying and like I said before a few more hours and she wouldn't be here. We caught the swelling in time and was able to relieve the pressure but there's no guarantee that your wife won't suffer some sort of brain damage."

"What do you mean she'll have amnesia?"

"She will have a lot of headaches, she may slip into depression, her communication and movement skills may or may not be limited. It will all depend on her when she wakes up."

"When do you think she will wake up?" I asked.

"Right now we had to put her in a medically induced coma to keep her still and allow her body to heal. With your permission we would like to keep her in that state for at least a month or until the swelling on the brain goes down."

"Can I see her?"

"I'm going to make an exception and allow you in the recovery room for a few minutes because your hand is requiring medical attention." I looked down and blood was on my clothes, on the floor and my bones really were sticking out. I didn't care I just needed to see my wife.

"Hi, I'm Samantha one of the nurses that will be taking care of your wife when she comes to ICU. Dr. Watson informed us that he gave you permission to see her for a few minutes." She walked me in a section of the room that she was in by herself and pulled the curtain back to give me privacy. I looked at her and broke down at the sight in front of me. CiCi had tubes everywhere and her skin was pale. She had bandages on her head, stomach area, hands and one of her feet. She was so skinny it looked like no one had fed her in months and what I could see of her hair it was messy and had blood all through it.

"CiCi baby you are safe now. I swear on my life that they will pay for what they did to you and my kids. I love you so much and I need you to fight and come back to us. I know you can hear me baby. We need you and I'm going to be here everyday waiting for you to get better."

"Mr. Thomas I'm sorry but they are going to be bringing her in a room and the doctor wants to get you prepped for surgery." The same nurse said. I nodded my head and kissed my wife on the lips. The machine started beeping fast causing the nurses to run back in.

"What happened?" Samantha asked.

"Nothing I just kissed my wife." She smiled as CiCi's heart rate started coming down.

"Well I guess whatever you said to her she heard you and she felt the kiss. Now hurry up and get that surgery over with so you can get back to her. You being here is going to help her get better faster."

"What's your name again?"

"Samantha."

"Thanks for saying that. I needed to hear that. Do me a favor?"

"What's that Mr. Thomas?"

"Can you stay here until I get back? For some reason I don't trust anyone else here with her. I don't know any of these nurses and after what she's been through I need to make sure she's safe."

"Sure. I get off at seven-tomorrow morning and it's only nine o'clock so you have a lot of time to do what you need to do. After you get the surgery." I don't know why but I gave her a hug and left my phone number with her. I told her if she had to leave call me first so I could send someone else up there. I had to leave but I had to make sure everything was in order with my kids and my hand first. This was going to be a

35

long journey, but I was going to be by my wife's side every

step of the way.

Iesha

I couldn't believe my mother would do some shit like that to my sister. I could see her doing that to me but not her. What did CiCi do to her so bad that not only had her kidnap my sister but cause bodily harm to her like that?

After Cream had his surgery, we all left and went to his house to get the kids some clothes and he packed a bag because he wasn't leaving the hospital until his wife did. My kids were so happy when they saw their cousins come through the door. They asked a ton of questions and Junior answered them all.

It was hard hearing him say my mother would take them outside, feed them, play with them but wouldn't allow them to see their mom until bedtime. I had to stop him when he went in the kitchen and grabbed a frying pan and demonstrated on one of Summer's dolls what my mom did to CiCi.

"Baby, I have to take Junior to see someone." I told Darius who was switching channels on the TV.

"My nephew is not seeing a shrink." He got out the bed and went in the bathroom. I waited for him to come out before I finished speaking.

"Darius, he's my nephew too. Do you think I want him to see a crazy doctor? No, I don't but he needs to. Look how he demonstrated what my mother did to my sister. That shit is not ok and he needs to speak to someone. Just as I said that we heard a scream down the hall. We ran into the room Cream was staying in because that's where I had Junior sleeping. He was in the corner with his knees to his chest crying. I ran over and hugged him tight.

"What's wrong Junior?" I saw Darius standing there pissed.

"I had a dream that grandma was hitting mommy again and she wouldn't wake up." Darius came over and picked him up and brought him in the room with us. After I went back to check and make sure all the kids were still asleep I got in the bed with them. Junior had the remote in his hand and turned on cartoons as he laid his head on Darius chest.

"What do you think now?" I asked him without saying too much.

"He'll be fine. I got him." I knew I was going to have to take the lead on this because he wasn't going to agree anytime soon.

"Is my mommy ok? I want to see her." He looked over at me.

"Mommy is fine. She is asleep right now so she can get better."

"Is she eating? You know grandma only gave her bread. I used to put snacks in my pocket for her when grandma wasn't looking." I listened to him talk about the torture his mom went through and couldn't stop myself from crying.

"Don't cry auntie Esh. You said mommy was better now right? And daddy is with her right?" I shook my head yes and wiped my eyes the best I could.

"You're right Junior. Daddy is going to protect her and me and uncle Darius are going to protect you, your sister and your cousins."

"But who's going to protect you?"

"Uncle Darius is." I told him and got comfortable in the bed.

"Well the Monster guy told grandma that he's taking you and my cousins away soon and no one will find you either." I covered my mouth and looked over at Darius who was out the bed putting clothes on. I already knew what he was about to do and jumped up. I grabbed his hand, took him in the bathroom and turned the water on so he couldn't hear us.

"Where are you going? It's the middle of the night." I asked him as he tied his timbs.

"I'm going out to find this nigga. There's no way I can have him plotting on you and my kids. Look what the fuck he did to my niece and nephew. Fuck that, look what he allowed your mom to do to your sister." I stood in front of the bathroom door trying to block him from leaving.

"Move baby." He put his hand behind me on the doorknob.

"No Darius. I don't want you out there and then I have to worry about if you're coming home."

"You know I'm not going to let him take me away from you." I didn't know what else to do so I did what I knew best and unbuckled his jeans and dropped to my knees.

"Fuck Iesha. Let me go. Shit baby." He took my hair in his hand and started making love to my face. When I felt him stiffening up I got up, pushed him back on the toilet and slid down on his dick and gave him a nice ride.

"Iesha I love the hell out of you. Keep going I'm about to cum."

"Me too baby." We both released at the same time and sat there trying to catch our breath. He lifted me up and stroked his man back to life, bent me over and had to cover my mouth to keep me from screaming.

"Shit Darius, Junior is in the other room." I told him throwing my ass back.

"Baby, this bathroom big as hell and the door is on the other side. Plus we have the water running he can't hear shit. Now cum all over your dick." He smacked my ass and I gave him what he wanted. After we finished we jumped in the shower and when we came out Junior was knocked out on the bed. Darius let him stay the night with us but told me I could look up some therapist in the morning and that he would let his brother know.

"Baby, don't think because you fucked the shit out of me that I'm not still going on the hunt for that nigga."

"I know you are but at least I kept you in for tonight." I leaned over Junior and kissed his lips.

It had been six weeks since my sister and the kids came home. Junior's nose was back to normal, Patience got her stitches out and CiCi was still in her coma but her body was healing much faster than the doctors expected. They said it was probably from Cream not leaving her side and I truly believed that. Those two were one in the same and him being there had her fighting to come back.

"Hey Nana and Pop Pop." I heard Summer yell out as I was coming downstairs. We have all been taking turns going up to see my sister. My father seemed to be taking it just as bad as Cream. He stayed at the hospital at least two to three times a week with him. For some reason he felt as if it was his fault no matter how many times we told him it wasn't.

"Hi Nana's baby." Ms. Thomas said picking Summer up.

"Nana, Patience is the baby now. I'm almost four." She and Junior were a few months behind each other in age, yet she thought she was the oldest out of all the kids.

"You will always be my baby." She kissed Summer and went to the kitchen to get something to drink. My dad sat on the couch and started watching cartoons with the other kids and Junior played on his new Ipad. Darius brought him a new one because the other one was at the house and he didn't want him to have any memories with it.

"I'm leaving dad. I will see you when I get back."

"Auntie Esh can I go see my mom today?" I wanted to say no but he hasn't been up there since the night they were dropped off there.

"I'm coming too." Summer said handing my dad her shoes to put on.

"Fine. Lets go." I put them in the car and drove to the hospital with the talking me to death. Oh my goodness. Whoever said kids didn't talk enough never met my daughter

43

and my nephew. The nurses knew who I was and didn't give me a hard time about bringing the kids up there but they did ask me not to have them up there long.

"Mommy." Junior ran over to the bed and Cream stood up and gave me a hug. He looked like shit. His hair hasn't been cut, he needed a shave and he looked tired.

"Daddy when is mommy going to wake up?"

"Soon Junior. Soon." I gave him a crazy look because she was still in the coma. Cream pulled me to the other side of the room.

"The doctor said the swelling in her brain is gone and that her body has healed quickly. They removed the cast off her foot today and her ribs and lungs may take a little longer to heal but otherwise she's doing good."

"Are you serious Cream?" I had tears running down my face and went over to the bed. Summer was lying on one side of CiCi and Junior was on the other side. I snapped a picture in my phone. I had been taking photos and videos of the kids for her since she's been missing so much.

"Her color is back and it looks like she gained weight."

"Yea, they've been pumping fluids in her through the IV and some other shit to help her get it up."

"Iesha."

"Yea. What's up?" I asked him brushing my sisters hair back softly. The bandages were off and you could see the hair growing over the spot they shaved when they had to do surgery.

"I told them to bring her out of the coma. I need my wife to wake up. Do you think I'm being selfish?"

"What? Hell no. I wish she could've come out earlier but her body needed to rest. Cream; don't ever think needing your wife is being selfish. The doctor told you she was ok and now its time for her to rejoin her family."

"Yea, but he did it yesterday and she still hasn't woke up." I could see him trying to hold back tears.

"Don't worry Mr. Thomas it's just a matter of time before she wakes up." The nurse Samantha said when she came in to change the IV bag. She told us we had to step out so she could bathe her.

A half hour later Samantha came to the family room and told us we could go back in. CiCi was lying there in a

45

fitted shirt with some gray sweatpants and some slipper socks.

Her hair was brushed back in a ponytail and she had a fresh

coat of nail polish on her nails. The entire room smelled like

that Pear lotion she loved.

"Thank you Samantha." I told her and gave her a hug.

Cream was paying her extra to keep his wife looking perfect

even thought she was in a coma and he looked like shit. He

said she would kill him if she woke up and he had her looking

a mess. We stayed up there talking to one another and I even

said a few things to CiCi.

"I love you mommy. Daddy said grandma can't hurt

you anymore and uncle Darius said he's going to kill the

Monster guy. You can wake up now." When he kissed her

cheek, we noticed her eyes flutter and Summer said she felt her

finger move. We called the doctor in and he told us that she's

ready to wake up but it's up to her.

"Mom is aunt CiCi going to wake up soon?" My

daughter asked on the elevator. I grabbed her and Junior's hand

when the elevator stopped and stepped off. For some reason

Junior stopped in his tracks and hid behind me when a woman went by us to get on. I told him to cut it out and keep walking.

I would ask him about that later because he was a very social person so to see him scared of someone had me worried. I didn't know if the appointment with this therapist would go well if he was scared of people now.

Tasha

When Monster took me out the basement that day and told me he dropped my daughter and her kids off at the hospital I was livid. It wasn't his decision to make so for him to go behind my back and do that had me rethinking our partnership. Especially since he knocked two of my teeth out.

He and I were not seeing eye to eye right now because he was dead set on taking Iesha and her kids, which I didn't have a problem with. But he wanted me to be the one to lure her to him. I keep telling him if I do it she won't make it to him because I'm killing her on site. Imagine my surprise when she walked right by in the hospital and didn't have a clue it was me. Junior had the nerve to pretend like he was scared of me. Yea I knocked the shit out of him but no one told his ass to call his dad. I bet he'll learn next time.

"Can I help you ma'am?" Some nurse asked me when I got to the floor CiCi was on. I only knew she was alive because Monster followed the gay guy on Facebook that worked in Cream's restaurant and all he talked about was his best friend

48

getting better every day. Of course, I'm here to make sure that doesn't happen.

"Yes, I'm here to see Cecilia Barnes." I saw here looking down on the computer.

"I'm sorry there's no one here by that name." I had been up there a few times before and this other nurse kept giving me a hard time. Telling me she could get her husband to come out and talk to me.

"Can you try Cecilia Thomas?" The moment I said that, she gave me a different look. It was like she knew I didn't belong there but still gave me the information.

"Yes, she's here. Her room is B216. It's straight down the hall, the last door on the left." I nodded my head and started digging in my purse for the syringe I had. I went to step inside and saw Cream coming out talking on his phone. I walked in the room on the opposite side that was empty and stood there until I couldn't see him anymore. I know he didn't leave because his keys were on the table next to his wallet. That meant I only had a few minutes to do it. I grabbed the IV part that the needle goes in and pushed all the serum inside it.

"If I didn't kill you the first time, this will surely do the trick." I whispered in her ear and stepped out quickly.

I walked down the hall with the biggest grin on my face. I heard a machine beeping and the nurse calling a code blue as I pressed the elevator doors. I looked down and realized I left the fucking syringe in the room. Oh well, that shit is in her system now. I got off the elevator and saw security running to the stairs and a few cop cars pulled up. Once again, I had the hospital on lock down but not before I got out this time.

"Now that's how you kill a bitch." I said into the phone when Monster answered.

"Oh shit. You went through with that shit?"

"Yup. One down, one to go."

"Crazy bitch. I'm not going to tell you again that if you lay a hand on Iesha that will be the last thing you do."

"Oh shut up. I don't know why you think she's going to leave with you willingly. You may as well get yourself ready for that heartbreak."

"Bye Tasha. Just know when you get here you better be prepared to suck this dick." For this nigga to be so in love with

Iesha he sure as hell stays fucking me. I stopped at the store to get a few things to make tacos for dinner. I couldn't believe how lucky I was again when I ran into Darius who was whispering sweet nothings in some chick's ear. I mean this chick was feeling all over him and he didn't seem to be hiding at all.

"I can't wait to ride that dick." I heard her say as I went down the same aisle on purpose.

"Oh yea. Then what are we doing in this store? We could be fucking in my car right now." He told her. I was laughing hysterically. That bitch Iesha must've had garbage ass pussy to have these men constantly looking elsewhere for it.

I searched the parking lot to see if I could catch them in the act but since I didn't know what he drove I was lost. I wanted to send that shit to Iesha so she could be heartbroken again. I don't know why I didn't take a picture while we were in the store. I brought the bags in and found Monster on the couch with his dick out hard as fuck.

"Get your ass over here and swallow these kids and then you can make my dinner."

51

"I love it when you talk to me like that." I gave my man what he wanted and after dinner; finished what we started. Yes, I claimed him as my man and I know he did the same.

Darius

Cream called me earlier and said he was getting CiCi moved to the house and asked me if I could meet the nurse over at the store to pick a few things up. We were at Wal-Mart in one of the aisles when she told me that the woman walking towards us had been to the hospital a few times asking about CiCi. I had no idea who she was. I told her to stand in front of me so I could get a better look at her without staring.

We pretended to talk shit to one another, and this woman stood there listening with her nasty ass. I wasn't worried about being caught with Samantha she was happily married with two kids. Her and Iesha had become very close since she was her sisters nurse.

"Are you sure that was her?" I asked trying to focus in on the pictures I snapped with my phone. I just hit the button over and over. I was going to ask Junior if this was the same woman that did this to them.

I drove straight to the hospital because Samantha was meeting Iesha over Cream's house so everything could be ready when she got there. He refused to have her lying in a hospital bed so he purchased one of those king sized memory foam adjustable beds. When I got there and went to her floor I saw him yelling at some nurse. There were doctors, security guards, cops and nurse standing around watching. I had to pull him away just to calm him down.

"Yo. What the fuck is going on? Why you yelling at her like that?"

"Because that stupid bitch allowed some woman to come in my wife's room without permission I may add. The woman stuck some liquid cyanide in her IV. If it wasn't for the person leaving the syringe in the IV, we would've never known why the machines were going off."

"WHAT? Are you fucking serious?"

"I know it was her mother but the person she described isn't her. Man I can't wait until we find this bitch. She is really testing me."

"Where were you?" I asked because he never left her side so I was shocked that this even happened.

"Damien called to ask me some shit about inventory, so

I stepped out. I walked down the hall to ask the nurse when the doctor was coming to discharge her when the machines started going off in her room. If she would've died, I swear everybody in this motherfucker would be dead right along with her." He started pacing back and forth. I saw Amir walk in with Louis and Maria behind him. Maria started packing CiCi's stuff up and Amir picked CiCi up and started walking with her to the elevator.

"Mr. Thomas we have to take her down in a stretcher. It is not hospital policy to take your wife out like that." One of the nurses yelled out. I saw my brother pull his gun out and point it at the nurse who let the woman pass.

"Don't worry about what the fuck I'm doing. What you need to be worried about is if I'm going to sue y'all dumb asses for allowing some stranger in here to kill my wife. Every one of you knew there was a list to see my wife; yet no one bothered to check. And you better hope I never see you again." He said to the nurse who was now in tears. I pushed him down the hall and onto the elevator.

"You bugging Cream."

55

"Fuck that stupid bitch. She almost had my wife killed." I wasn't going to waste my time arguing with him about it. I was the same way when that bitch tried to kill Iesha.

We pulled up at his house and the nurse and Iesha were waiting with the door open. After Amir laid CiCi down we all went downstairs and left my brother alone with her. I already knew he was going to feel more comfortable with her at the house. The doctor that was caring for her at the hospital was making a house call twice a week to check on her.

"Darius we are going to stay here for a few days. I brought over clothes for all of us and the kids already decided which rooms they were staying in." Iesha said. I didn't say anything because once her mind was made up that was it. We ordered the kids pizza and rented the movie Kung Fu Panda 3 since they loved the first two. We were all in the living room when Cream finally came down.

"Iesha can you put her night cloths on? I feel like I'm too rough when I touch her."

"Boy you're not worried when y'all being fresh." She said going upstairs making us laugh.

"You ok." I asked him when he sat down next with us.

"Yea I'm good. This shit with they mom is crazy. I mean if she don't want to fuck with them that's one thing but she's trying to kill both of them."

"Uncle Cream I can't hear with you and daddy talking." My daughter Lyric said.

"Ok Lyric. I'm sorry." She went and sat on his lap and put her finger on his lip and said no more talking. When the movie was over Cream was knocked out on the couch. I told the kids to be quiet and that it was time for bed.

"Baby let him sleep. I'm going to stay in the room with CiCi tonight so she's not alone. I know he will have a fit if he wakes up and she was."

"That's fine but first come take care of me. If I'm going to be sleeping alone, I need something to put me straight to sleep." I slapped her ass, locked the house up and made love to my woman. I can't imagine what he's going through and I don't want to. When her and Kelly almost succeeded in killing my girl and my daughter, I lost it.

Cream

My wife has been home from the hospital now for almost two months and she was still in a coma. You couldn't tell unless you knew because I made sure Samantha and Iesha kept her looking good. Today Patience was turning one and we decided to have cake and ice cream with just the family. I didn't want to throw a party and her mom couldn't be there.

I got in the shower and let the hot water beat down on my skin. I found myself thinking about my wife and how I used to make love to her. I stroked my man and erupted all over my hand. No matter how horny I was I would never cheat on her again. This was going to be my release until she came back to me.

I washed myself up and stepped out the shower only to find that I left the towel on the bed. I dried off and put some sweats and a t-shirt on to join everyone. I bent down to kiss my wife like I did every time I left the room. This time I felt her kiss my lips back. I jumped back and saw her staring at me with a slight smile on her face.

"It's about time you came back to me." She lifted her arm and wiped the tears from my eyes.

"I wasn't going to miss my daughter's birthday." She whispered but I heard her. I lifted the covers off and picked her up. She pointed to the bathroom and when I got her in there she pointed to a toothbrush and toothpaste.

"CiCi you can't stand right away. Your ankle was broke and the doctor said you will need physical therapy for a little while."

"I know baby. I heard everything. I even heard my mom tell me since she couldn't kill me at the house she would do it at the hospital."

"You already know what's about to happen to her." She nodded her head letting me know she understood. She stood up on one foot and tried to limp out and almost fell.

"You are hard headed. Come on. Let's go make your grand entrance." I picked her up and carried her down the stairs. No one paid me any mind because we had already discussed her being in the living room in the recliner. I know it seems crazy but just because she wasn't awake I still wanted her to experience it even if she could only hear.

"I want to sit on the couch James." Oh how I missed the way she said my name. I put her down and the first one to notice she was awake was my daughter. She crawled over to her, climbed on her lap and started kissing her. Again no one was paying her any mind until Junior jumped on the couch and started yelling she was awake.

"Oh my God CiCi. When did you wake up?" Iesha yelled and came running over with tears in her eyes. They hugged and before I knew it everyone was in the living room. Her dad wouldn't leave her side the entire night and my mom couldn't stop crying.

"I love each and every one of you. I listened to you talk to me, I heard you cry and Junior I'm so proud of you for being a big brother to your sister." She started crying which made every female in the house cry.

"Where's Samantha?" I heard her ask. She made her way over to CiCi and kneeled down in front of her.

"I want to personally thank you for everything you did

for me. From bathing me to making sure I still looked good for my husband. You gave me all kinds of pep talks to wake up and you kept my husband from killing a few people. You went above and beyond for me and you didn't have to. God has a special place for you and I will forever be in debt to you." Samantha was hysterical crying as my wife gave her a hug. We had the cake and ice cream but CiCi didn't want any of it. She said her stomach wasn't ready for all that yet. The only thing she wants to eat was some chicken noodle soup.

"Baby are you ok." I whispered in her ear as she laid in the tub. When she didn't answer I got a little nervous and said it louder causing her to jump.

"Why are you yelling?"

"Did you hear me?" When she shook her head no I knew it was something wrong. I spoke in her left ear and she heard me fine but when I spoke in the right one she didn't respond unless I spoke loud. The doctor said she may lose hearing in that ear. I washed her up and carried her back into the room.

"The doctor is coming by tomorrow to check you out.

And I have to get you to a ear doctor to check you hearing."

"I'm fine James."

"I know that, but he still has to check you out. He's also set up physical therapy for you too."

"Whatever."

"Stop being like that and just do what the doctor ask please." I kissed her lips and laid down next to her.

"I love you James Thomas."

"I love you too Cecilia Thomas." A few minutes later I heard her snoring and I was right behind her.

The next day the doctor was coming around ten so I had Samantha come over at 8:30 to get her ready. She claimed she didn't need Samantha as much anymore, but I still wanted her around until she was fully able to do everything on her own.

After the doctor left the physical therapist came and worked with my wife for about an hour and left a wheelchair for her to use until she was stable enough to use a walker. Of course, CiCi wasn't trying to hear that but she agreed. I love her to death, but I'll be damned if I'm carrying her all around the house.

CiCi

I can't believe the lengths my mother went through to try and kill me and to hear what she did to my kids had me pissed because no one could find her. I lost a lot of time with my family along with a child and my hearing. When I found her she's going to wish I were never born.

I didn't tell my husband, but I had been browsing online to find different ways to torture my mother. I really didn't hold too much ill will towards Monster because James killed his sister and even though he let my mom torture me I understood his reasoning. Its still no excuse for what he allowed her to do and James would kill me if he heard me say that.

Today was my last day of physical therapy whether the therapist agreed or not. For six weeks I've been going through it and I feel fine. I don't think I'll ever be able to walk without a limp because whatever happened to my ankle was so bad I have metal plates in it. I also been working out as much as I can without standing. I've been doing my leg, stomach and butt exercises to get my body tight like it used to be. Iesha told me the kids were spending the night at her house so that James and I could go out on a date.

"Damn, girl I see you trying to get fucked tonight." Iesha yelled out walking in my room. I had on a tight dark blue dress with spaghetti straps that criss crossed in the chest area. My hair was in pin curls to the side covering up the part I had surgery on and my makeup was done to perfection. I wore the diamond studs with the necklace to match that I got from him yesterday.

"I'm scared to have sex with him sis. I don't know if ill be able to please him like I used to."

"Bitch, are you serious? That is your husband and there's no way in hell he's going to look at you different if you can't." She rolled her eyes and passed me my black red bottoms from the closet.

"I know but it's been so long and what if?" She cut me off before I could finish.

"Bye CiCi. Your man is waiting downstairs. Don't put your shoes on until you get down there. You know that ankle

65

isn't used to walking in heels."

"I know. I hope I can keep them on to walk. Maybe I should grab my slippers."

"Sis, stop being nervous. That's your husband not somebody you just met. He's going to love you even if you went out in sweats. Just relax and have fun." I shook my head and grabbed her hand for her to help me down the steps. James had his back turned talking to Junior when I came down.

"Mrs. Thomas you are the most beautiful woman I've ever seen and I'm glad you're my wife." He said when he turned around.

"Thank you baby. Is it too much?" He kissed my lips because we tried to keep it PG in front of the kids.

"You're perfect." Iesha and Samantha were standing there with tears coming down their eyes.

"Why in the hell are you two crying?" James asked and they both flipped him the bird. Samantha was like a sister to Iesha and I now. Her husband and kids have been to the house so many times and the guys get along with him great. James helped me put my shoes on and walked me down the stairs to the car. He drove us to New York and we ate dinner at some expensive ass restaurant. Afterwards we stopped by the wax museum and took a few pictures. We didn't stay long due to my ankle. He had me take my shoes off and put on my slippers so we could take a walk on the beach at Coney Island. He put his jacket down for me to sit and sat behind me.

"Baby, I thought I lost you. When you went missing I knew you didn't leave me but I couldn't find you."

"James, I would never leave you and I'm glad you never gave up looking for me. I know you feel like you failed when you found out where we were but don't feel like that. We put that house up for sale and there was no way anyone would've thought we were there." I wiped the few tears that he had coming down.

"I know but as a man it was my job to protect you. I don't know why I didn't send anyone to follow you back home that night. I knew his ass was in town but I didn't think he would kidnap you."

"Let's not talk about that right now. The only thing that matters is that we're home safe and sound." I lifted up to kiss him and he pulled back. He helped me up and we walked back to the car.

I thought we were on our way home until he pulled up to the Ritz Carlton hotel. We went to the Penthouse suite and I was shocked. There were black and gold rose petals throughout the suite with candles to match. There was a bottle of Champagne on ice and a silk see through negligee on the bed with a balloon that read I love you floating over the top.

"James when did you do all this?" I turned around and he pulled me close and made love to my mouth so good I almost had an orgasm. He undressed me slowly and kissed each part of my body starting from my mouth, down to my neck, my shoulder, my breast and my stomach. I had juices leaking down there and he hadn't even sniffed my pussy yet. I went to sit down and he stopped me.

"I want to try something different baby. Do you think you can stand a little longer?" I shook my head yes.

He put my hands up against the wall and spread my legs open. I felt his tongue snake in and out my ass and he took turns doing the same to my pussy. He put two fingers inside and I swear all my bodily fluids came rushing out. He sat back against the wall and pulled my body closer to his and devoured my pussy like it was a steak.

"Keep that shit coming CiCi. I'm thirsty as hell and only you can fill me up." I was fucking his face against the wall until I couldn't take anymore and my knees buckled. He laid me down and climbed on top putting his mouth on mine allowing us both to taste what I gave him. He tried entering my treasure and I tensed up.

"It's ok baby. It will hurt but you know your husband got you." I nodded my head and started to relax. Once he was all the way in we became in sync.

"Fuck CiCi I missed you so much and this pussy so tight. I can't hold it any longer." He started twitching and came right away.

"I'm sorry. Shit, it's been a long time."

"If you would've lasted any longer I would be asking questions. Now lay back and let your wife take care of you." I covered his pole with my mouth and had him back to life in no time. I had him moaning like a bitch but I didn't want him to cum yet. I wanted to remind him of why no other woman was made for him. I slid down on his dick and squeezed my muscles together as I went up and down on it. I got on my feet and started pounding harder and faster.

"Ride that shit CiCi. Show me how much you missed it." The way he was talking was driving me insane. He sat up and sucked on my chest as I rode him and continued talking shit and slapping my ass at the same time.

"Turn over CiCi. I want you off your feet now." I did as he said and to say he fucked the shit out of me from the back, he fucked the shit out of me.

"Just like that James. Oh shit baby, I'm cumming again. Right there. Yes, yes yes…"

"Fuck I'm about to get you pregnant tonight. Take this dick baby."

"Oh God James. I love you so much. I'm about to cum again."

"Here I cum CiCi. I hope you get pregnant. Aww shitttttt…" He came so hard we just laid on the floor.

"You still have the best pussy ever. Don't ever let me hear you say you hope you can please me like you used to." I rolled over to face him.

"Yea, I was coming up to see if you were ready and I heard you and sis talking. CiCi I don't ever want you to think that. You are my wife, my soul mate. No other woman can make me feel the way you do. Don't ever forget that."

"I know but its been a long time and." He cut me off and kissed me passionately. We made love off and on all night until I finally tapped out and told him I couldn't take anymore. I was 100% sure I got pregnant.

Monster

This entire kidnapping thing with Tasha is starting to take a toll on me. Not because I recently found out she was Iesha's mom but the constant obsession she has with killing her. I get the reason she doesn't like her but what their dad did didn't have anything to do with her.

Now, I have to monitor everything her stupid ass does to make sure she doesn't kill her. I've been following Tasha everyday since she assumed she killed CiCi at the hospital. Her dumb ass left the syringe in the IV, which told them someone tried to kill her and was able to save CiCi.

Nobody knew I followed Damien on Instagram or Facebook because I was under a different name. He was also fucking with my cousin who I used to smoke with every few days. Yea, my cousin was what most people would call a homo thug. He was 6'2, dark skinned and had a body that the women yearned for. Yet, he was bi-sexual, but if you ask me, he was fully gay.

I mean he was definitely in love with the Damien dude. I could tell by the way he spoke about him and how he had him living with him in his mini mansion. Yup, my cousin worked for Cream and Darius trafficking guns and made a pretty penny. If they ever found out I'm sure his ass wouldn't be on this earth much longer.

"What up cuz? What brings you on this side of town?" My cousin Arvin asked when he opened the door. I stepped in and noticed how the shit was laid out. I'm not about to describe what his house looked like; just know the shit was something I wanted me and Iesha to live in with all our kids.

"Not much. Just haven't seen you in a while and came by to smoke." He led me to the living room and passed me a blunt that was already lit.

"Yo Monster. Tell me the shit aint true." He said flipping through the channels.

"What shit?" I passed him back the blunt and slouched down in the chair getting comfortable.

"Why my dude told me you kidnapped not only my bosses wife but his kids?"

73

"Something like that."

"Come on man. What the fuck was you on? And how you did his kids was fucked up?"

"Listen. I never laid my hands on any of them. That was all their mom and her psychopathic ass. She came to me with some plan about doing it so she could get closer to Iesha. At first I wasn't with it but then I thought fuck it. If this could get me my girl back then I'm down.

Anyway, the first day I admit I let her beat CiCi's ass because she claimed she deserved it. But then whenever I would leave the house and come back she would fuck her up even more. Finally I was over the shit and planned on dropping them off at home. But I get to the house and find out this bitch is really Iesha's mother and I had been fucking her the entire time."

"Get the fuck out of here." He was shocked and amused.

"Yup." I finished telling him the entire story and that's when I found out he was at the hospital that night because he had cut his finger trying to cook for his dude and needed stitches.

He told me how Damien called up his boss and gave him the information but that he left because he didn't want Cream or Darius to know he was with him. Even though people on the streets may know how he got down he wanted to keep that part of his life away from his boss. I could understand, it wasn't their business anyway.

"What are you going to do? You know there's a bounty on your head. I'm surprised no one saw you."

"I know man. I'm just trying to get my family and get the fuck out of here."

"Your family? Monster I'm going to keep it one hundred with you. Iesha and her kids are not your family. Whatever the two of you had in the past is just that. The past. Darius proposed to her before everything happened and she said yes. Not only that; their families security is so tight it's like they are both the presidents wives. You won't stand a chance trying to get her." I sat back listening to what he said but I had my own plan. I wasn't going to tell him just in case he decided to run his mouth.

"Hey baby. How was work?" He asked the dude who came in and sat down beside us.

"It was good baby. I'm tired as hell though. James gave me a promotion and now I'm the club's manager. Wait, who is this?" He stared at me.

"This is my cousin Monster." I looked at Arvin's stupid ass and shook my head. He just told me how tight Damien was with the girls and gave him my damn name. I could see him smirk and start typing away on his phone.

"Arvin, I know this is your cousin but I'm about to be a rich bitch because of him."

"What are you talking about?" My cousin asked looking at him.

"This is the same nigga who tried to kill my girls man, then he kidnapped your bosses wife and kids and trying to go for Iesha. If you think I'm about to sit here and allow him to walk out of here after what he did and he has a two million dollar bounty on his head you are sadly mistaken." Before I could say anything, I heard a noise and felt a burning sensation in my arm. I looked down and this motherfucker shot me. I jumped up out my seat and tried to tackle this nigga. Arvin jumped up and stood in between us.

"Yo what the fuck Damien?" I heard Arvin ask as I watched the blood pour out.

"Fuck that Arvin. You should be ashamed of yourself allowing him to sit here knowing what he did. If James and Darius ever find out you'll be floating in the river with him. I can't take that so you need to decide right now if it's him or me." I couldn't believe he was giving him an ultimatum and I was his blood cousin. Shit, our moms were sisters.

"Sit your dramatic ass down. You know me better than that." It was at that exact moment, I knew my cousin sold me out. The one thing I know about him is that he's always been a loyal nigga. Once I heard the knock at the door I took off running to the back.

"He's in the back. Hurry up before he gets away." I heard Damien yelling. I didn't know who I was madder at Damien for shooting me or my cousin for ratting me out.

All I know is I had to make it out of here alive. Shit, Iesha was waiting on me. I could feel myself starting to lose consciousness due to the amount of blood I was losing. I didn't have anything to stop the bleeding. I heard niggas talking in the background and before I could go any further I heard him.

"Here is this stupid motherfucker right here." Whoever the person was dragged me by both of my legs through the grass. I could feel my back getting scraped as we hit the pavement in the front. I was thrown in the trunk of the car and that was last thing I remembered.

Darius

"Wake the fuck up." I yelled at him as he sat there naked and barely breathing. I had him sitting here for the last few days. You could see the boiling hot water tearing away at his flesh when I threw it on him. He opened his eyes and I smiled because I'm sure this is the last place, he thought he would be. I thought about calling my girl and CiCi over to handle him, but I wanted answers first.

After he gave me what I needed they could do whatever to him. He wiped his face and tried to cover his dick with his hands. No, I didn't have him tied up because I felt like that was a sucker move. People always tied their victims up and I never understood why. Its not like they could escape or even kill you. Shit, not only was he naked but he had no weapons and with the amount of niggas here, he wouldn't be able to do much anyway.

"Listen Monster. You already know I'm not into that talking and torturing shit. I just want some answers and the fate that awaits you will come shortly after."

"I ain't telling you shit."

"You don't really have a choice."

"And why is that? You're going to kill me whether I tell you or not. I'd rather die knowing that Tasha is still out there and she's going to finish what she started. You see I may not have Iesha in the flesh but once her mom gets to her I will have her in death." I sat in the chair across from him studying his face and even though he tried not to show it I saw nothing but fear in his eyes.

"You did all of this for my fiancé?"

"She won't be your fiancé for long. Her mom is gunning hard for her and she won't stop until she sees Iesha lying in a coffin. If I were you, I would be spending as much time as I could with her." He started laughing, which was pissing me off more. As much as I wanted to fuck him up, I was saving that moment for my girl. The door opened and in walked my cousin and his two guards. I saw his eyes grow wide as hell like he saw a ghost.

"So this is the infamous Jeremy that slept with my wife and then raped her." Yes, my cousin Miguel was the one who had Monster followed over to his cousin Arvin's house.

Monster slipped up and kept the same cell phone he used when he slept with Miguel's girl. He kept it off, therefore we couldn't track him. Fortunately, for us he turned it on to get in touch with Violet; claiming he was coming out there and wanted to hook back up.

She played along with it until he was able to trace the call. His dumb ass stayed on the phone with her until he went into his cousin's house. Not too long after we got the call from my cousin did I receive a text from Arvin and Cream got one form Damien telling us they had Monster at his house and was waiting for what to do next. Those two were worth keeping on our team.

"Whoa. Raped her? Bro, your chick gave me the pussy for free; there was no need to rape her." Miguel punched him so hard,m teeth flew out. After a few minutes, hot water hit him again.

"If you didn't rape her then why did I get the ransom letter stating you enjoyed spending time with her and how the sex was a bonus?" Miguel was standing in his face with his fist balled up like he was going to hit him again. The door opened before he answered and Cream walked in.

"Man, I don't need to rape no bitch." Miguel hit him with a two-piece again knocking him to the ground. We had to grab him back because we didn't want him dead yet.

"You're so stupid man. That note was a setup from your ex Faith." Miguel walked back over to him and squatted in front of him.

"What the fuck is you talking about?" We all stood there listening because this nigga was knee deep in shit over here in the states; and in Puerto Rico. How the fuck did that happen. He started rambling on about how him and Miguel's ex Faith have been fucking for a while and that she was the one who tried to kill Violet with the truck. What he said next had us all in shock.

"You better get home to your new wife. They are plotting against her as we speak."

"Tell me what the fuck you know; NOW." Miguel said with his hands around his neck. We had to remove his hands in order for him to speak.

"You're over here in the states thinking I raped her when the person who did it is right under your nose. You think all the people you have working for you are loyal? Nigga, you better think twice. Faith has been working with someone who has wanted your spot for years. He is coming to claim what he said is rightfully his; including your wife." I saw the look in my cousin's eyes and I knew he was about to murder everything moving over there.

"When we are finished over here, trust that Puerto Rico is our next stop. I'm tired of people coming for our family." Cream told him and we both gave him a hug before he left.

"Why the fuck did you do my wife and kids like that?" Cream yelled out. His nose had to be broken from the way my brother just hit him.

"I didn't do that shit."

"But you didn't stop it either." Cream continued beating on him until it looked like he wasn't breathing.

"I want our doctor friend to come and nurse him back to health." I could see the weird look on everyone's face as I said it.

"Don't look at me like that. This nigga tortured my sister in law and kept her and the kids away from us. Its only right to show him the same courtesy." I said. I saw one of the guys get on the phone and call the doctor. It was just a matter of time before he got better and then it would be the girls' turn to handle the situation.

"That's right." Cream chimed in and left.

That night I got home and found Iesha sitting in the dark waiting for me. She had tears in her eyes as she stared at me take my shoes off. I already knew why she was mad and didn't want to get into it but I know it was coming.

I sat there for about twenty minutes and when she didn't say anything I got up and took a shower. I felt the cold air from the curtain opening. She hugged my waist and her hand found my manhood and stroked him to life. No words were spoken as she turned me around and bent over. She and I went at it in the shower until the water turned cold. I wrapped the towel around her and we both dried off and laid in the bed naked.

"Is it over?" She asked rubbing the side of my face.

"One down, one to go."

"Which one is down?" When I told her it was her ex she turned her back to me.

"What's wrong? I thought you would be happy we had him." She turned back around.

"I am but I wish it was my mother. I hate that we're getting married in a couple of months and she's still walking around. I find myself paranoid all the time now and its because I have no idea what she looks like. At anytime, she can attack me and I won't see her coming."

"Iesha, I'm not about to let your mother do you like she did your sister. Plus, the one that planned on kidnapping you is locked away waiting for you to handle him."

"Baby, I don't want to see him. If my sister does, then that's fine but you can do whatever you want to him." I was shocked that she didn't feel the need to dispose of him herself but if that's how she wanted it I was going to tell Cream in the morning and see where he wanted to go from there. If his wife

didn't want any parts of him you can guarantee I'm about to

make him take a dirt bath ASAP.

Iesha

When Darius came home a week ago informing me they had Monster, I was happy but upset at the same time. I believed he deserved what was coming to him, yet; my sister said he didn't lay any hands on her.

I told him I didn't care what he did but since he was still alive I was going to take a ride over to the spot where they had him in hopes of finding out where my mother was. I needed to hear for myself why he went along with my mother. Darius said he had a meeting this morning, which gave me time to speak with my ex alone.

The drive over had my mind in overdrive because I wasn't sure what I would be walking into. People can say what they want but this man was about to be my husband. Did I still have feelings for him? No. But I wanted answers and CiCi only gave the bare minimum to me.

Cream told me she would tell in due time but fuck it I didn't want to wait. I pulled up to the spot, turned my car off and sat there for a few minutes. I had to get myself mentally ready to face him. I knew he was going to die and this would be the last time I saw him. I opened the door and he was lying on what looked like a stretcher with an IV in his arm.

"Good morning Ms. Iesha." The doctor said. I spoke and watched him walk away as I walked towards Jeremy. He turned over and reached his hand out for me. I moved my hand back and pulled a chair up next to him. I could tell someone beat the crap out of him from all the bandages.

"Hey baby." He whispered with a smile on his face. I couldn't believe he really assumed this was some sort of social call.

"Jeremy, I'm only here because I need answers." He turned away from me like he had an attitude.

"Look, I know I'm about to die and I welcome it because you won't be too far behind me once your mom finds you." My mouth hit the floor when he said that.

"What do you mean when she finds me?" He proceeded to tell me all the plans my mother had for me. I was flabbergasted at the horrible things she wanted to do.

"Where is she Jeremy?" He refused to tell me and that was pissing me off. How dare he be mad at me when he put himself in this situation?

"I'm not telling you shit. If I can't have you now then I'll have you in death. That's what I told your fake ass fiancé too."

"You have to get over this obsession with me. You and I had our time together and you messed it up."

"Yea, but when we slept together after I came back I knew you still had feelings for me and he was holding you back. Iesha, I swear if you get me out of this we can take the kids and leave. No one will find us and we can be together like we used to talk about." I shook my head listening to the nonsense he was spitting. This nigga was delusional if I say so myself.

"There will never be a me and you in life or death. I was wrong for sleeping with you when you came back knowing I had a good man at home."

"A good man huh? Didn't that nigga cheat on you again? How can you take him back but not me?"

"For one we didn't go years of not speaking or talking once we broke up. Two, I slept with you before he cheated and three NIGGA YOU WERE SLEEPING WITH A MAN." I had to yell the last part out. I didn't know how much clearer I needed to make that known.

"Yes I did. I told you that was a one-time thing but you still slept with me."

"You're right Jeremy, I did. I'm not going to lie; when you came to Darius house,m you were looking fresh to death. You were the old Jeremy I fell in love with and I wanted to see what you came to town for. Fortunately, for you, I had a weak moment, which in return caused a lot of turmoil in my family. You are partly the reason my sister and her kids went through the shit they did. But you know I blame myself too because I should've never slept with you."

"Don't say that. You know as well as I do that you enjoyed it." He had the nerve to grin as he said it.

"Jeremy, we will always have memories but me getting you out of here and us running away together is not going to happen. I'm about to marry the man of my dreams and there's nothing you or my mom can do about it. Yes, she's gunning for me but you can bet a bitch will be ready and waiting. She will not catch me slipping ever again." I was cocky when I told him that knowing damn well I wasn't confident because we had no idea what she looked like.

"I will see you soon and when I do we can sit back and watch over your so called fiancé and how he will move on right away."

"I'm not leaving him anytime soon. You on the other hand are going to meet your fate sooner than later. I know Darius wanted me to wait for my sister but today is your lucky day. There won't be any more stalling or allowing you to breathe any more of our air." I picked my purse up and pulled out my new 9 mm out and put it to his head.

"So this is what it came down to? I didn't expect you to be the one to pull the trigger and end my life."

"It's only right." I told him and watched his brains splatter all over the warehouse. I felt someone come up behind me and take the gun out of my hand. I turned around and fell into his arms.

"It's ok baby. It had to be done." I shook my head and looked up at him. I loved this man with everything in me and I knew if Jeremy lived he would cause nothing but problems for us.

"How did you know I was here?"

"Iesha, I know it was a matter of time before you came to get your closure. Why do you think I kept him alive so long? I can't take away what you and him had together because that was in the past. There were things that you needed him to answer. Baby, you did what you had to do."

"Everyday you remind me of why I made the right choice becoming your wife."

"I'm the man of your dreams Iesha?"

"Without a doubt. I knew it the first day we met, even though I gave you a hard time."

"You are the woman of mine as well baby girl. Don't ever forget that. I love you."

"I love you too Darius. I'm ready to go home."

Darius carried me to his truck and ran back in to tell them what to do next I guess. Cream called and he told him what happened. I heard my sister telling him to drop the kids off because I needed time to deal with what I did. I was ok but I guess they didn't think the same thing. Darius ran a bath for me and lit some candles. I was relaxing when I felt him climb in behind me.

I let my headrest on his chest and listened to his heartbeat. He and I were meant to be together and I'll be damned if I allow anyone to mess up what we have. My next goal is to find my mother and I'm going to stop at nothing until I do. I know she's out there watching and waiting but I'm going to catch her slipping; it was just a matter of time.

Tasha

I've been calling Monster's ass for the past week but he wouldn't answer. I know he was mad because he couldn't get to Iesha but I had a plan to expedite the shit. No one knew but I ran into someone that's going to bring heartbreak to that stupid nigga Cream and I couldn't wait. I never had a problem with him and I actually loved him for my daughter.

However, that punk tried to break my arm and was brainwashing my daughter not to allow me to see my grandson. Therefore, it was only right to make him suffer and I plan on continuing to make his life hell.

When I found out CiCi wasn't deceased I blew a gasket. I was in the mall shopping for a new lingerie outfit to show off for my man when I saw her and the kids with him and four big dudes behind them. I already knew getting to her again was going to be next to impossible. It didn't matter as much because I had fucked CiCi up pretty good and the damage was going to last forever in her mind. She wasn't like Iesha where she could move on and forget about it.

The best part about my new face is no one knew who I was and I could move around without being paranoid. CiCi no longer worked, which I knew, was coming because he never wanted her to anyway. I did find out that she was doing some interior designs for private investors. That was my way of starting off my new plan to fuck Cream's perfect family up. It was a matter of time before Darius world comes crumbling down. He was so far up her ass he wasn't going to see shit coming either.

Most people will call me a bitch and tell me to leave them alone and let them be happy. Unfortunately, I don't have a nice bone in my body anymore. After their father died I think I died with him. Yes, I was sleeping with someone else and I killed him but he was still my everything.

Sometimes I lay in the bed thinking about him and what we could be if he was still here. Then I remember he was leaving me for that bitch and let me know I did the right thing. If he wasn't going to be with me; he wasn't going to be with anyone else. Now I'm sitting here waiting for my new project to arrive.

I met this person when I spilled coffee on him by accident coming out of Dunkin Donuts. He was tall, brown skinned, dreads and a smile that would make any woman's panties wet. I apologized to him and he offered me to have a seat with him inside. We sat and talked for a few hours so imagine my surprise when Cream and CiCi stepped inside and he couldn't keep his eyes off her. I made sure to keep my head down so she wouldn't notice me. They didn't stay long and I was happy just in case she recognized me.

"Damn, I miss her." He whispered but I heard him.

"Excuse me." I said trying to make sure I heard him right even though I knew I did.

"Oh nothing. I saw someone that I used to deal with."

"Let me guess. It was the woman that just walked out with her man."

"Yea. I thought they were over but I guess not." I could see the hurt in his face but I was ecstatic. This shit was going to crush Cream's heart and I couldn't wait. I sat there and let him vent to me and if I didn't know any better I would say he was in love with CiCi. *Oh, the shit just keeps getting better and better.*

"I really just want to talk to her and see what happened."

"What if I told you I could get you close to her." His face lit up like a kid in a candy store.

"Oh you know her?"

"Yes, I do."

"Why didn't you speak when she was in here?"

"Let's just say you and I have something in common when it comes to that man of hers. Do you want to meet up with her or not?"

"Hell yea."

"Give me your number and I will send you a text of when and where? But you have to be ready because she doesn't stay out long."

"I heard about what happened to her. I wanted to be by her side but I knew her man wasn't going to allow that."

"Don't worry. When you see her it will be just the two of you." He paid for our coffees and walked out. All I had to do now was figure out how I was going to get the two of them in the same room. Everyone who knew my daughter was well aware of how in love she was with her husband.

I wanted to make their meeting as intimate as I could. I got to the apartment Monster and I shared together and went to work on the perfect plan. I sent his ass a message and when he didn't respond I wrote his ass of. I wasn't into chasing any man but my ex husband and he was no longer among the living.

CiCi

When I stepped in Dunkin Donuts with husband, I felt someone staring at me. I glanced over my shoulder and we locked eyes. He was sitting with some woman whose back was to me. He smiled and I put my head down because James would kill him if he saw that. He was always over protective of me but since the shit with my mom happened and the fact we couldn't find her made it was worse.

I quit my job on my own but I'm sure he was happy. I didn't want to have two bodyguards with me at my job because people would start asking questions and my business is my business. I was doing a little interior designing for people but nothing big. It had to go through James in order for me to do it and of course I had security.

"You ok baby?" James asked. I felt myself feeling a little flushed. I just wanted to leave and get far away from that man as I could.

"I'm ok. Can we leave?" He kissed my lips and we left; leaving our order. I laid back on the headrest thinking about how he and I ended things.

"Hello." His voice was still sexy as hell. I sat on the phone and listened to him repeat himself before I spoke. I wasn't sure if this was the right thing to do but I had just found out my husband cheated on me and I needed to vent to someone who didn't know what was going on.

"Hello, can I speak to Malcolm?"

"Speaking. I didn't think I would ever hear from you again after your man threatened me." I smiled at the thought of him remembering my voice.

"Yea, well things have a way of working themselves out."

"How are you CiCi?" When he asked me that I just broke down crying.

"Where are you? Let me come to you."

"No, I will come to you. Send me your address." We said our goodbyes and before I knew it I was pulling up to his house. He came out and helped me in the house and waited for

me to speak. Over the next month I would visit him whenever James had Junior. He and I became close and decided to give it a try and be together. I knew it would be hard because I hadn't gone to a divorce lawyer yet. Malcolm was very understanding and didn't pressure me at all.

"Let me make love to you CiCi." He whispered in my ear as we sat as his house watching a movie and molesting each other. I didn't say anything and lifted my shirt over my head. This man made love to every part of my body and I couldn't get enough. Every time I would go to his house we would attack one another and have sex.

"I'm in love with you CiCi." He told me as we laid in the bed after one of our sex sessions. I didn't know what to say because my heart was still with my husband. No, I wasn't sure if we would ever get back together but I know I wasn't in love with Malcolm either. I cared about him and had strong feelings for him but only one man had my heart.

"Malcolm, I'm flattered but I can't say my feelings are the same. You know I'm still married and I thought we were just trying this out until I got divorced."

101

"I can't help that I fell in love with you. CiCi you're telling me you have no feelings for me."

"It's not that. I do but I'm not where you are. Maybe we need to take a break. I mean I jumped into this because I needed comfort and you were there. I appreciate it to the fullest but I wasn't looking for what you are right now." I started getting dressed without saying another word. I left the house that day and never spoke to him after that. A week later I found out I was almost three months pregnant. I knew for a fact it was James because I never had unprotected sex with Malcolm and I was too far along.

"You sure you're ok? You've been acting weird since we left Dunkin Donuts." James asked again when we got back to the house.

"I'm ok baby." I pulled his face close to mine and stuck my tongue in his mouth. He let his seat slide back and told me to lift my skirt up. I slid my panties off and glided down his pole slowly and went to work. The truck was rocking, the windows were fogged and our moaning could be heard throughout the driveway I'm sure. People can say what they want but I was never leaving this man. I craved him and depended on his love and sex.

"I love you James. No one will ever take my heart from you." I moaned in his ear. He pushed me up to look in my face.

"What's wrong?" He wiped the lone tear that escaped my eye.

"Nothing baby. I'm just happy to be back." I know it was my responsibility to tell him right then since it was on my mind but that was in the past. Plus, there was no need because I was never going back to Malcolm.

"CiCi, I'm your husband and I can tell when something is bothering you. I'll be right here when you're ready to talk about it." I didn't say anything as I slid my skirt down.

"Lets take this inside. You know that was just a tease." He laughed and helped me out the truck.

I was sitting in the office downstairs when my email popped up with a person wanting me to do a consult on a home they were moving into and if I could do it today. I was shocked to receive them because no one had my personal email address and they usually go through James. I responded and told the person to send me the address. The house was about twenty minutes away and I told them I'd meet them within the next hour.

I got to the house and it was beautiful with a long driveway. I was going to have fun designing this one. I grabbed my stuff out my car and walked up to the door and knocked. At first it took a few minutes for the person to answer. To say I was shocked when he opened the door would be and understatement.

"Hello CiCi." I backed up and attempted to get in my car. The security was at the end of the driveway so I doubt they saw me trying to get away.

"Wait CiCi. Please, I just want to talk to you. I don't like the way we ending things. The least you could do is tell me why."

"I don't have to tell you shit Malcolm. How dare you set this up? This is my business and I don't appreciate the games." He stood there with his arms folded and a grin on his face.

"Just come inside so we can talk. I swear you can leave right after." I was a bit hesitant but I know he wouldn't hurt me. I stepped in and just like I thought it was beautiful. I glanced around and this man had a candlelight table set up. There was food under a tray but I didn't know what it was because it was covered. I turned around and his lips found mine. I immediately pushed him off me.

"What the fuck Malcolm? You said you wanted to talk." He pointed to the chair for me to sit.

"CiCi, I'm going to get straight to it. I miss you and I want you back." I took a sip of water before I spoke.

"Malcolm, I'm with my husband and I'm never going to leave him. What we had was special I can tell you that but it's in the past. You have to move on."

"Don't you think I've tried? You are everything I want in a woman and I had you but you went back to the same man that cheated and broke your heart. I would never do that to you." He lifted his drink and took a sip.

"That was my decision to go back. I'm sorry if you thought we were going to be more than we were but its never

105

going to happen again." I felt my throat getting dry and started drinking more water.

"Where's your bathroom?" I asked. I felt myself feeling flushed and threw water on my face. The next thing I remember was waking up in bed naked with Malcolm.

****

"Oh my God how the hell did I end up in bed with you?" He had this sneaky grin on his face. I began dressing so fast I had to slow down because my shirt was on backwards.

"You don't remember. You came out the bathroom and were all over me. Then told me you needed me to make love to you so it would remind you of what we used to be." He spoke with confidence making me think I really said that. My head was pounding and I could hear my phone ringing from the other room. Then the banging on the door started which let me know James sent security to come get me. I opened the door and the sunlight was basically blinding me.

"Are you ok Mrs. Thomas? Mr. Thomas said he's been calling you and you didn't answer."

"I'm ok. I had my phone on vibrate while I was working. Can one of you drive my car and take me to my sister's house?" He shook his head and helped me get in the truck. I called my husband and told him I was ok and called my sister and told her to open the door.

"What's wrong CiCi? Are you ok? Let me call Cream."

"NO." I screamed out making her hang the phone up. She gave me an odd look and stood there with her arms folded.

"Where is everyone?" I asked lying down on the couch. When she told me no one was home I felt a relief. I had to tell someone what happened. She sat there with her hand covering her mouth. She knew that Malcolm and I messed around while James and I were separated. She went into the kitchen and brought me back a bottle of water and some Advil. After I took it, she called James and told him to come pick me up.

"Iesha I can't tell him. He's going to kill him."

"Who the fuck cares Ci? I know you don't want to believe it because you two were together but he slipped you a roofie or something."

"No I don't think he would do that. What would be the purpose when we've slept together before?"

"Ci it doesn't matter that you were together before, he knew you wouldn't give it to him willingly so he took it." I knew she was right but I didn't want to see it that way. James came not too much longer and we drove home on silence. I got out the shower and went to lie down and found him sitting on the edge of the bed.

"Where were you CiCi?" The way he asked me had me scared to respond. He had his head down looking at the ground with his elbows on his knees.

"I went to an appointment to do a consultation for a house." He scoffed up a laugh and I swear it was scary.

"I'm going to ask you one more time. Before you answer I want you to think about it first." I stood my ground and told him the same thing.

"I think it's best for me to stay away from this house for a while. Don't call me unless it has something to do with my kids."

"What? You're leaving? What is going on?" He walked over to me and yanked my head back and stared in my eyes.

"I asked you where you were because it's not like you to disappear."

"And I told you." I yelled out trying to take his grip off my hair.

"You did tell me. But tell me where it states that going for a consultation requires you to come back with two fucking hickeys on your neck?" He tossed me to the bed and slammed the door as he walked out; not giving me anytime to answer.

I jumped off the bed and ran to the bathroom. How could I not notice that shit? I looked around and didn't see any until I lifted my hair up. This motherfucker put two gigantic hickeys on the back of my neck. I was at a loss for words. I tried to call James over and over, but his phone went straight to voicemail.

I fell into the bed crying because I didn't know what to do. My so-called friend slipped something in my drink, which by the way was only water and my husband think I cheated on him. Well technically, I did but not willingly. What the fuck? I just got my family back to the way we were after the shit with

my mom and now it's fucked up all over again.

Cream

I knew something wasn't right ever since the day we walked out of the Dunkin Donuts. I brushed it off as paranoia because we still couldn't find her mom. I hear from my wife a few times a day so when I didn't, I assumed she was asleep.

After a couple of hours, I noticed she still hadn't called so I called back and still no answer. I hit up the security dudes and they told me she was at a house doing a consultation. I thought that was weird because I didn't have anything set up nor did anyone check the house before she got there. I was on my way to the address when she called and told me she was ok and headed to her sisters.

She looked out the window on the drive home like something was weighing heavy on her mind. I was going to get to the bottom of it. I glanced over her as we sat at a red light and had to do a double take because I know my eyes had to be playing tricks on me. I moved her hair from the back of her neck and pretended to massage her neck when I wanted to snap it. My wife, my soul mate was sitting next to me with two huge hickeys on her neck. I had to keep myself calm at the moment. As she took a shower I sat there debating with myself about leaving.

She looked me dead in my face and lied about where she was. I know I cheated on her but it was to keep her out of jail. No, it wasn't right but I thought we moved past that. Did she do this on purpose? Was this payback? Did she give her body to him like she did with me? My thoughts clouded my mind and I felt a tear fall and wiped it away before she came in the room. I could see in her eyes that she was terrified of me at the moment and that's why I had to make the decision to leave. If I stayed with her any longer, I don't know what I would've done.

I laid in the bed listening to the banging on the hotel room door. I refused to move and sat there staring at the ceiling. I heard a beep and the door opened with my brother and Louis standing there looking at me. They glanced around the room and shook their heads. Darius opened the shade and it was so bright I felt like a vampire.

"What the fuck is going on bro?" Louis asked sitting on the bed next to me. I hadn't spoke to anyone about what happened.

"Yea nigga. It's been two weeks since we heard from your ass." Darius said standing over me.

"I'm good. I just needed some time to myself."

"We know. Mom told us but you haven't seen your wife or your kids." Soon as he said that I found myself getting pissed all over again.

"Fuck CiCi." Louis and Darius glanced at each other then back to me.

"You don't mean that shit bro. What's going on?" Louis asked again looking down at his phone.

"Oh I guess when you went to check on me she didn't tell you. Well let me fill you in on your sister in law. The bitch cheated on me."

"Yea right." Darius said shaking his head.

"Oh but she did. The day I picked her up from your house she claimed she was doing a consultation but came home with two hickeys on her neck." Neither one of them said a word after I told them that shit. We all sat there in silence for a few minutes when Darius phone rung.

"He's good. I'll be home in a few." I heard him say as he hung up.

"Did y'all have a talk? I mean what did she say when you confronted her?" Louis asked me.

"She couldn't say shit because I left. If I didn't get out the house I probably would've killed her."

"Damn. Well let's get you out of here. Mom wants us to come to the house for dinner." Darius threw some clothes at me and told me to get in the shower. I turned my phone on and my notifications exploded. I figured they were from CiCi. I would check them when I got dressed.

Once I finished, I paid my hotel bill and decided to stay at my old condo. I was still refusing to go home. Call me childish but I wasn't ready to deal with it yet. The thought of someone else making her moan or even touching her made my skin crawl and had me pissed every time I thought about it.

I opened up my messages and they were all from her begging me to come home and saying we needed to talk. I made one stop before I got there; if she wanted to play this game then I was going to join in. I stepped in the house and all eyes were on me. My son and daughter came running over. I picked them up, kissed their cheeks and put them back down.

"Who the fuck is this bitch?" Maria yelled out with Iesha standing right next to her. I saw CiCi turn around and we locked eyes. For that second, I wanted to take her upstairs and make love to her but it left my mind just as fast as it came.

"Don't be rude you two. This is Denise and she will be joining us tonight as my date." I looked around to make sure my kids didn't hear me say that. I saw CiCi wiping her face and run out the dining room. I gave zero fucks at this point when it came to her feelings. At least when she found out I cheated on her I cut that shit off. I fought hard to get my family back and her ass is probably still hanging out with dude so its fair game if you ask me.

"Let me talk to you son." My mother told me to meet her in the other room.

"What the hell are you doing?" My mom got straight to the point.

"Ma, CiCi and I are no longer together. She is with someone else so I would appreciate it if everyone gave my date some respect."

"Respect James." I turned around and CiCi was standing there wiping tears from her eyes.

"Yea respect. Something my wife, excuse me, soon to be ex-wife didn't give me." She mustered up a laugh.

"Is that what you think? You think I don't respect you?" I nodded my head.

"Where was the respect when you went behind my back and made a deal with the fucking devil? Huh? Where was the respect when I asked you over and over if you had someone else and you denied it? Or when you slept with her with no condom and still came home and slept with me? Where was the respect then? Where was it when you decided to bring this chick up in here?"

"You know that I made a bad decision when I cheated but it was for you."

"It was for me?" She threw her head back laughing.

"Are you serious? Each time you stuck your dick in her it was for me? Each time you gave yourself to her it was for me? Keep telling yourself that."

"I thought you were over it but I see you're not. Why does it matter who I brought here, when you're clearly having the time of your life with that other nigga?" I found myself getting mad looking at her.

"You would think that. Why didn't you just ask me what happened with him?"

"Ask you for what CiCi? When I asked you that night where you were, you didn't tell me. Why would I assume you would tell me anything else?"

"You know what James, Cream or whoever you are today. I'm over this shit with you. You're going to believe what you want no matter what I tell you but remember this." She opened the door to walk out.

"It may have taken me a while, but I took you back after you cheated. James, I will always love you but I can see we won't ever get back to where we were. There's too much hurt on both our parts."

"You're right, we won't. Enjoy your new life with that nigga." She left out leaving me there with my mom and in my feelings. She did take me back but I don't think I could do the same.

"James, let's get through his dinner and we'll talk some more tomorrow." I nodded my head at my mom and followed her back in the living room. Everyone was sitting at the table and had started eating.

Denise was still standing by the door waiting for me. I grabbed her hand and sat her next to me. I saw that CiCi was missing but kept my mouth closed. After dinner my son came and sat on my lap to tell me something.

"Mommy said we were staying with you tonight before she left."

"That's fine. I'm going to drop my friend off and I'll be back to get you." I told him and had him go watch TV. I sent a text to CiCi and told her to have a bag ready for the kids. I didn't want to go by the house but I had no choice. I didn't have anything at the condo and couldn't get anything until the morning.

"I contacted your lawyer and he said the divorce papers can be done as early as tomorrow afternoon." She said handing me the bag and slammed the door in my face.

I didn't know what to say. I knew I didn't want to be with her right now but divorce wasn't in my vocabulary at all. I put the bags in the back seat and drove to my condo.

I got the kids ready for bed when I noticed Denise sent me a text thanking me for the dinner. I turned my phone off and went to bed. I didn't know what was in store for CiCi and I but being together was not in our future right now.

Denise

The night Cream called me up and asked me out to dinner. At first I was shocked since I hadn't heard from since he had broken up with Kelly. I met him bartending at his nightclub one night. He and I started conversing at the bar when she walked in making a spectacle of herself. I could tell he didn't appreciate all the attention she was causing because he had security escort her out. A few minutes later he sent someone to find me at the bar and they brought me upstairs. Needless to say, he was the perfect gentleman and didn't try to get fresh with me.

He and I went out on a few dates and come to find out him and his brother owned the bar and had plans on opening more. I was impressed with the fact he wasn't some drug dealer who just opened the club to hide money. I swear that's all I heard these men were doing. I'm not knocking their hustle but why does ever come up have to be off of them poisoning the community with drugs. The night we had sex was the last time I saw him.

"Damn Denise, I may have to lock you down. You got some good shit in between your legs." I grinned and went to kiss him. Usually he would back up but not this time he actually welcomed it, which had us having more great sex.

"I'm ok with you locking it down. I think I've fallen in love with your dick game." He smacked my ass and continued pounding in and out of me. This man had me gone off his sex more than any other man I had ever been with. When we were done he went in the bathroom and came out panicking.

"What's wrong Cream? Is everything ok?" He sat on the edge of the bed with his head in his hands.

"The fucking condom broke." He said barely above a whisper. I didn't know why he bugged out like that.

"It's ok Cream. It was only one time and I doubt anything even made it in." I came up behind him and massaged his shoulders.

"I'm just not ready for kids right now. I want them with my wife; whoever she may be."

"I understand. Let's not think about that right now." It wasn't much we could do at the time but pray I didn't get pregnant.

The next few days I called him over and over but not enough to call it sweating him. He never answered so I wrote him off and that was fine with me. I ended up at the club a few months later with my sister hoping to talk to him but when he saw me, he ignored me.

I found out that he had fallen madly in love with this woman and she was all he saw. That was the last time I saw him up until two weeks ago when we ran into one another at the store. We said hello, exchanged hugs and kept it moving.

It had been a few weeks since he took me over to his mom's house for dinner and I hadn't heard from him. I knew the moment we walked in the house and the two women questioned him it was going to be a problem.

I saw his wife in the kitchen with his mom and I had to give her props. She was gorgeous and seemed to be glowing. When he introduced me, I saw her run out and his mom said she needed to have a word with him. I could hear him and his wife arguing and I'm sure everyone else could too because the chick Maria turned the music up. I didn't move from the spot I was standing in. I'm far from a punk but I wasn't going to allow these two women to jump me either.

The dinner went better than I expected except for the two chicks not speaking to me. Everyone else seemed to be cordial and the kids kept asking who I was.

"Hey. Thanks for letting me stop by." Cream said walking in with a bottle of red wine in his hand.

"You remembered." I laughed looking at the bottle.

"Yea." He smiled and took a seat on the couch. I could see him looking around at all the toys and the game system.

"Oh you got a man I see." He lifted the game controller up as he said it.

"Not anymore. He and I broke up a little over a year ago. I'm riding solo." I started getting nervous because he came earlier then he said and my house wasn't the way I wanted it.

"Sorry to hear that. Who's game is this then, if you don't mind me asking? No man is going to leave this type of game system here." I had to laugh at that. Men were very protective of their game systems and so was my son.

"That's my son's." I saw him raise an eyebrow.

"Oh, I didn't know you had kids. How old is he?" *Fuck he was asking too many questions now. Get it together Denise; it's only a question.* I had to tell myself.

"He's five and a half."

"Ok. My son just turned four and he is a piece of work as you can see. And he's the same way with his ipad that your son is with his video game."

"Yes, he's definitely a cutie pie. He is going to be a heartbreaker when he gets older." I said sipping on my wine.

"Yea. His mom said she doesn't want him having any hoes around him. So where's your son?"

"He's out with my sister. She picked him up an hour ago and took him to Iplay America over in Freehold. He loves that place."

I went and grabbed my phone to send a text to my sister but he snatched the phone out my hand and put it on the table.

He said he wanted my undivided attention and by the way the wine had me feeling now he was sure to get it.

Cream started kissing on my neck and instead of pushing him away I welcomed it. He and I were both trying to rip one another's clothes off. He picked me up and carried me upstairs. I directed him to my room and he shut the door with his foot. I know he was going through something with his wife but shit a bitch was horny. That was his problem not mine; she isn't my friend. The minute he entered me I came right away.

"Shit you tight as hell. Turn over." I got on all fours and started throwing my ass back. All that could be heard was our skins smacking. Not too long after we both exploded and fell back. He took the condom off and I heard him flush it down the toilet. I guess it didn't break because he came back in fine.

I moved down to his shaft and put my mouth around it bringing him back to life. He stared down at me doing it and smiled. That had me feeling like I was the shit and I went to work.

"Fuck, I'm cumming." I let him cover the inside of my mouth with his seeds. He had me come back up and straddle him. When he came back to life again he slipped a condom on and fucked me straight to sleep. I heard someone knocking on my door and looked over to see he was still lying there. I put my robe on, walked downstairs and opened the door.

"Hey mommy." My son yelled giving me a hug.

"Ummm did we disturb you?" My sister asked.

"Shit. I was supposed to text you and ask you if he could stay with you and Chris Jr. Cream snatched the phone." She put her hand up before I finished my sentence.

"Cream who?" I gave her this look that she knew who I was talking about.

"Bitch are you crazy. What if he sees him?" She whispered.

"I know. Can you take him to your house?"

"Wait. He's still here?" I shook my head yes.

"I'm telling you right now if his wife and her sister come over her I'm shooting both of them. Those bitches aren't anything to fuck with and you're sleeping with her husband. What were you thinking?"

"I know. We were having drinks and we ended up sleeping together."

"Fine. C.J. come on let's go." My son came running down the steps with his backpack and put his controller in his bag.

"Mommy, why is your bedroom door closed?" He asked. I never have my room closed.

"I must've closed it by accident. Have fun with your aunty. I'll see you tomorrow." After they left, I jumped in the shower and felt him come in behind me. This man must've needed sex because the way he and I were having it, I was so tired I felt like I ran a marathon. He stayed the night but was gone before I woke up the next day. I didn't feel any kind of way. I knew it was just sex and probably the last time I saw him and I was ok with it.

Iesha

I couldn't believe my sister and Cream were really going through with the divorce. I tried to get her to tell him what really happened with Malcolm, but she said let him believe what he wanted.

It was fucked up that she took him back after he cheated but he couldn't find it in his heart to do the same. Then come to find out he was dealing with that Denise chick heavy. I found that out by accident because Darius told me he had to meet up with Cream before him and Denise went out of town. If I didn't know any better I would say they were messing around before the shit happened with my sister.

Tonight, I was having my bachelorette party at the nightclub. Darius wasn't having a bachelor party because he wanted to monitor my shit. I didn't tell CiCi they were going to be there. She is my maid of honor and I love her to death but I know she wouldn't come. She tried to stay far away from him as possible and now that she was pregnant her emotions were at an all-time high. She pulled up at my house and blew the horn. I gave the kids a kiss and walked to her car.

"Ok CiCi you look nice." She had on a black sweater that came down on both of her shoulders with a pair of jeans and some black ankle boots. Her hair was out and parted down the middle. Her makeup was always on fleek and she was blinding me with all her jewelry.

"Ugh, are you trying to catch one of these strippers attention?" I asked putting my seatbelt on.

"Yea right. I'm not thinking about any man right now. I'm already in a fucked up situation with my soon to be ex-husband." I looked over to her and saw the tears coming down her face. We pulled up at Maria's and when she got in she knew something was wrong.

"CiCi, I love you to death but don't waste anymore tears over that motherfucker. He is out there doing him and even though you can't right now you have to show him you're stronger than you look." Maria told her and kissed her cheek.

"She's right sis. You've been through hell and back and you're still standing. Show him what the fuck he's missing." I let that last part slip out.

"I already knew he was going to be there. Come on you two didn't think I thought he wouldn't. That's his bar too; why you think I stepped out looking as good as I did? You never know I may give a stripper my number. I may be pregnant but I won't be forever." We gave each other a high five and picked Samantha up before we headed over to the club.

We got out the car and walked in the club looking like the sexy bitches we are. There were a lot of women inside waiting for the strippers to come out. Most of them I met when I would get behind he bar and I had flyers promoting it. I always found ways for my man to make money and these women were already in here drunk.

We made our way to VIP and I didn't see any of the guys yet, which was fine with me. Cream and my sister haven't seen one another since the night of the dinner and that was two months ago. Anytime he wanted to see the kids she would bring them to my house and he would drop them back off at

130

my house. She hadn't told him she was pregnant yet because she didn't want him thinking she only told him to break him and his new chick up.

We were on the dance floor when the guys walked in and I can't lie they all looked good. Boss was written all over them and the women were drooling. I noticed Cream staring at CiCi and she turned her head and went back to dancing. I was proud of her for not running to the bathroom or breaking down. Maybe he would see she didn't need his ass.

The strippers came out and the women went wild over them. One stripper in particular eye fucked the hell out of CiCi during his entire set. The song Pony came on and he found his way over to her and the lead stripper came to me. Shit, this niggas dick was so big I was scared to even look at it.

The guy moved on from me to the next chick, but all eyes were on CiCi and the other guy. He had her straddling him on his lap. She turned around and bent down to touch her toes in front of him. When she came back up he pulled her closer to his chest and his hands roamed her entire body. He turned her around and she jumped in his arms and he pretended to be fucking her.

I could see Darius and Louis laughing at Cream who was standing there pissed off. CiCi allowed him to lay her down on the ground and before anyone could say anything he was on top of her grinding like they were fucking. That shit must've thrown Cream over the edge because he came storming down the steps.

We stood up, pushed the stripper back and helped CiCi off the ground. I wasn't expecting my sister to grab him closer and stick her tongue down his throat. She was really putting a show on and I couldn't do shit but give her props. That's what his ass gets.

"Yo, take your ass home right now before I kill everyone in this motherfucker?" I heard Cream yell in her ear. She snatched away from him and went to sit back down. He lifted her up and carried her upstairs with all of us following behind them.

"That shit was so much fun. Y'all should've let me finish." She was feeling herself. I heard a loud crash and it was Cream tossing a bottle at the wall.

"Um what's wrong with you?" I asked with my arms folded.

"You think that shit is cute CiCi?" She laughed at him making us all look at her like she was crazy. I've never seen him this upset but when I did she would be the one to calm him. Knowing there was no calming him down, there was no telling what was about to happen.

"Oh you didn't like that Cream." She was pushing it. He hated when she called him that.

"You were basically fucking him on the dance floor."

"And." She was not backing down from him.

"And…" Once he started laughing, I looked over at Darius and Louis and they gestured for me to get her out of there. That was always a sign that he was about to tear shit up.

"Let's go sis. The strippers are gone and it's after three anyway. My wedding is a week away and I still have a lot to do."

"Fuck that. Oh y'all think because he did his signature laugh, I'm supposed to be scared." She walked up in his face.

"This nigga can't hurt me anymore than he already has. There's nothing he can say or do that can top what he did and is now doing."

"What the fuck you talking about?" He barked.

"You really think I don't know you fucking that bitch you brought to the house?" He ran his hand over his head but why? He decided to dip out. Why does he seem concerned about it hurting my sister?

"Or that I didn't know you fucked her before we got together? You're so fucking stupid, I bet you didn't know that's your son she has either."

"Nobody has kids by me but you." I saw nothing but confusion in his face.

"The next time you go over there to put your dick in her mouth and wherever else, take a look at her son."

"You don't know what you're talking about."

"I'm going to say this and then I'm leaving." You could see she was about to break.

"That is your son because he is a spitting image of James Junior." She started digging in her purse.

"I was going to wait to give you these, thinking we could work it out but I see that's never going to happen." She took some papers out and threw them in his face.

"And the next time you see me with a man or even dancing with one, stay the fuck away from me. You have no jurisdiction over this pussy and what I decide to do with it. Fuck you." She smacked the hell outta him, shocking all of us because she doesn't even fight like that. We ran behind her and you could hear him shouting about something.

"Sis is that really his son?" I asked when we got back to the house. She showed me a few photos of him on Facebook and she was right he looked just like my nephew. There was no way Cream could deny him even if he wanted to. People don't believe me when I say it, but when you want to find something out Facebook will give you what you're looking for.

"Damn. What are you going to do?"

"Nothing. That's not my problem."

"Yea but the kids are related."

135

"Iesha, you know I would never mistreat a child. I say I don't have to worry about it because we're not together. If we were then of course I would make it my business to make him a part of our life. That was before my time but since we're not together I don't have to do shit." I understood what she was saying. Shit, I been there, done that.

CiCi

James had some motherfucking nerve trying to come for me knowing he was out there doing God knows what with that bitch. I really shouldn't call her a bitch because she didn't do anything to me and my beef was with him. I dropped my sister off and jumped in the shower only to come out and find his dumb ass sitting at the edge of the bed. *I have to get the locks changed first thing tomorrow.*

I ignored him and moved around getting my pajamas out the drawer. I put on my clothes, turned the TV on, the light off and got under my covers. I let his ass sit there and bask in his thoughts.

"I didn't know CiCi."

"I don't care James. That doesn't have anything to do with me."

"This is how we treat each other now?"

"James, you have been treating me like this since you thought I cheated on you."

"Thought you cheated. You did cheat on me." I didn't have time to entertain his shenanigans.

"If that's what you think there's nothing I can say."

"You had two hickeys on your neck. I didn't put them there. Even if you didn't sleep with him, you allowed him close enough to do that." I sat back listening to him go on and on. I was tired of going back and forth with him over it. Yes, I could've told him the truth but I let him think he what he wanted. We weren't getting back together so why did it matter.

"Why are you here James? It's late and the only thing open after two am is legs and mine are not. So whatever it is you wanted could've waited until tomorrow." I was trying to be tough talking to him but I wanted him to hold me. I wanted him to make love to me and tell me we could get back together but that wasn't going to happen.

"I'm not giving you a divorce."

"WHAT?" I sat up on the bed.

"You heard what I said. I'm not about to let you be with some other nigga." I laughed at how stupid he sounded.

"Will you listen to yourself? You're out here flaunting your new woman, taking her on vacations out of town and you want me to stay married to you. I don't know about her but I wouldn't allow my man to do that."

"She's not my woman. We are just enjoying one another's company." He must think I'm stupid.

I snatched my cell off my dresser and logged into Facebook. I clicked on her page and handed him my phone. I saw him looking at all the pictures and start shaking his head.

"Now what were you saying." There were pictures of him at her house, when they went out of town, a few holding hands and some kissing. The last one she posted said missing my man but he's celebrating with his brother for his wedding.

"You're really feeling her huh?" He stood up and came to where I was now sitting.

"She's not my woman."

"James, you only kiss a woman if you're claiming her and it's clear as day in this photo that you are." I showed it to him again just in case he missed it. He let his hand run down his face and blew his breath out. This always told me that he was trying to think of what to say.

"No need to speak on it. I'm not mad."

"CiCi, I never meant to hurt you. I didn't know you were friends with her on Facebook."

"I wasn't. She friend requested me the day after you brought her to your mom's house. I didn't know why but I'm not petty so I accepted it. I think it was to let me know her son was yours." I saw his facial expression change from upset to angry.

"Why didn't you tell me?"

"For what? James, I've had time to think about everything that's going on and you and I are not good for one another. You believe I cheated on you and instead of asking, you accused me. Yes, I lied because I didn't know how to tell you what happened because I went on a consultation you didn't know about. You didn't waste any time finding someone else to occupy your time though; throwing anything we had away."

"Ok, maybe we are together but she knows how I am over you and have never overstepped her boundaries. CiCi it doesn't matter who I'm with, no woman will ever come before you or my kids."

"James, I really don't care anymore. I don't doubt you love me but you're falling for someone else and I understand."

"Come here." He lifted me up off the bed and stood me in front of him. He cupped my face and I allowed him to tongue wrestle with me. I felt myself leaking instantly. He kissed my neck and sucked on each of my breast making me moan out. I was wrong knowing he just said they were together but it felt so right and I couldn't stop him. He reached my stomach and looked up at me.

"We're going to discuss that when I'm done." He put his mouth on my clit and stuck two fingers inside. My body shook violently; releasing backed up juices.

"Fuck James. Make me cum again." I grabbed his head and pushed his face inside my pussy like I wanted him to jump in. The feeling he was giving me was long overdue. After I came a few more times he entered me and fucked me silly. He laid on his back and asked me to ride him.

"Fuckkkkk CiCi you are the only one that can fuck me like this or make me say your name." I stood up and dropped my pussy harder and faster on his dick.

"Shitttt CiCi. I love you."

"I love you too James. Oh my God, here I cummmm.." We both let go at the same time. I fell on top of him and listened to his heartbeat just like old times.

"How far along are you?" He asked moving my hair out my face.

"Four months." I looked up and he was smiling.

"I guess I got you pregnant when we went away." I shook my head and got up to clean myself off.

"Now what James?" I asked when I went back in the room.

"What do you mean?"

"You have a girl. This can never happen again." I told him.

"What do you want CiCi? If you want me; I'll leave her. If you want to work it out and still live separate I can do that too. It's all up to you." He had me on his lap kissing my neck. I was about to answer when his phone rang again. It had been going off non-stop since he came over. He looked down at it and hit ignore again.

At this moment, I didn't know what to do. I told him I had to think long and hard about the options he gave me. He went to leave and his phone went off again.

"You should answer it. She's probably worried about you."

"I don't care what she has going on. I keep telling you she won't ever come before you."

"What if its about your son?" I guess he thought about it because he picked the phone up.

"Why are you calling me back to back like that?" I couldn't hear what she said because the volume was down. I guess he learned his lesson form the previous time. I grabbed water out the fridge and opened the front door for him to leave. He hung the phone up and shut the door.

"James you have to go." I said as I felt his hands roaming up my body and found their way to his favorite spot.

Needless to say, he didn't go home that night and has been here ever since; that was a week ago. The only reason he was leaving today was because of the wedding. He didn't even want me to stay the night over my sister's house with the wedding party.

****

"I'll see you at the altar." He whispered in my ear as he continued hitting my spot. If he didn't want to go back to his chick I can't do anything about it. At the end of the day he was still my husband until the papers were signed.

"Did you hear me CiCi?"

"Yes. Oh shit yes. Baby right there." I came for the third time and he still had yet to cum himself. It was getting late and both of our phones were ringing off the hook. I got on top and rode him until he came so hard his toes curled. I went to kiss him and he asked me to give him a minute.

"No woman is going to make you cum the way I do. Remember that." I sashayed my ass in the shower and left him laying there. When I came out he was still in the bed.

"Hello." I answered my phone.

144

"Yea. Hold on." I passed the phone to James.

"Alright man damn. I'm coming." I heard him pouting in the phone. He hopped out the bed and in the shower. He threw some sweats and a t-shirt on because his suit was at the hotel with his brother.

"You're right. I've never had a woman fuck me like you and I'm not about to allow you to do that with another man either. I don't care what you say; getting a divorce is out the window and I'm coming home after the wedding."

"What about your girlfriend?"

"I broke up with her already."

"When? You been here everyday."

"The day I left out for an hour to go to the office I called her to come there. When she did I ended it. You know I can't be with two women at once."

"Oh."

"Oh my ass. You are the only woman I want and when this wedding is over I want you to tell me what happened the night you came home with those hickeys. If we plan on moving forward we have to put it all out there." I nodded my head and

145

kissed him before he walked out the door. Just when I started

trying to forget what happened he wanted to bring it back up. I

guess it needed to be said if I wanted him back.

Darius

Today was my wedding and I couldn't wait for my bride to walk down the aisle and say I do. Unfortunately, we were all waiting on my late ass brother to come. Now that him and CiCi were basically back together they were fucking like rabbits as always. I don't even know why he broke up with her anyway. They both cheated on each other and should've just gotten over it. That's why I loved my girl even more. She is definitely my ride or die and she stuck by me when she didn't have to. I messed up twice with her and I knew if a third time happened I would lose her for good. That's why a bachelor party was out of the question.

"Damn nigga. You couldn't stay away from her for one night?"

"You know how we get when we make up." He laughed putting his suit on. Louis and I just laughed because we did know how they got down. If it weren't for my wedding, we probably wouldn't see them for another week or so.

After we finished getting ready, we walked down to the limo and I swore I saw that woman from the grocery store. I wasn't taking any chances and told security that if their name wasn't on the list they were not getting in. I didn't want any of them coming to me saying this person was at the door and wanted to come in either. Same thing went for the reception; we had to make sure both girls were safe as well as the kids.

We arrived at the church ahead of the girls and sat in the limo taking shots. The driver opened the door and when we stepped out it was cold as fuck. I knew the weather was supposed to be a tad bit cold but it was brutal out here. We went inside and people were in line getting their names checked off on the list. It was good to know security was on point. I would hate to have to body someone at my wedding but I will. I saw CiCi come out the room holding my nephews hand.

"James your son wants you." She handed him off to my brother and went to walk away but he grabbed her.

"I love you Mrs. Thomas and we are still going to have the wedding of your dreams."

"Really. We can still have it?"

"Whatever you want you can have. You know that already."

"Ok, we'll talk about it later." They gave each other a kiss and she went back in the room.

"You two are sad." I told him following behind in the other room.

"Nigga please. When you and Iesha first got back together, we didn't hear from y'all asses either. Just because she was on birth control and didn't get pregnant doesn't mean we didn't know y'all were screwing like rabbits too."

"Whatever."

"Yea. That's what I thought." He said dapping it up with Louis. An hour later I watched my wife walk through the church like the angel she is. We both said our own vows and shed a few tears. The reception was even better because everyone was having a good time; even the kids.

"I love you Mrs. Thomas." I whispered in her ear.

"I love you to Mr. Thomas."

We danced all night long and I was ready to get on the plane and join the mile high club. Iesha had to give all the kids kisses over and over like she was never going to see them again. They were staying with my mom and the nannies were going to be there too.

When we returned from our honeymoon over in the Dominican Republic it was back to work. I called Cream and he filled me in on the new building he was opening called Cecilia's. No one knew about it yet because it was a surprise. CiCi kept talking about wanting to expand her business so he brought a building to do it. Next door was going to be Esha's. It was going to be a soul food restaurant with a little bit of Italian in it. It sounds weird but the menu was to die for. We had been working on this project for a year now and all we were waiting for was the CO to go through and we could start furnishing it.

"What's up bro?" I asked walking in his office.

"Nothing nigga. I just hung up with your ass."

"I know. I wasn't sure if there was more you needed to tell me off the phone."

"Well I do want to ask you something?"

"What's up?"

"Remember when CiCi said that Denise had my son." I nodded my head.

"Do you know she still hasn't brought that up to me yet?"

"Ok. Are you going to say something?"

"Nope. If she wants to continue acing like he isn't mine then I'm going to let her. I don't need any problems in my life. I feel like the minute she tells me all hell is going to break loose. It's best I act like I don't know."

"That could be your son though."

"I know but what if he's not? You know I take care of my kids but I'm not forcing her to do anything. He doesn't know about me and if CiCi didn't figure it out I wouldn't know. I'm just going to see how it plays out."

"I guess. But if I was you I would find out sooner than later." I know he didn't want any problems but if that's his son he had to do right by him. I was about to make a call to my mom. If anyone can talk to him besides his wife she could.

Cream

Today the guy from the city was meeting me at the building to do the inspection and grant me a CO for CiCi and Iesha's business. I got there and he was already in his car waiting. We shook hands and I gave him a tour of both spots that he passed with no problem. I sent a text to my brother and gave him the go ahead to set up dinner reservations for the four of us.

We were going to furnish it but the girls would probably change it all up so why not just let them do it. I put the alarm on my car and walked back into my office. The knock on my door brought me out of the nasty thoughts I was having about my wife. She sent me some naked pictures earlier and I was more than ready to go home.

"What's up Damien?"

"Some chick is here requesting to see you."

"Who is it?"

"I don't know but she was rather rude so I had to let her ass have it in a nice way." I stood up and followed him downstairs. I glanced down at the bar area and it was Denise and some other woman. I assumed it was her sister due to the resemblance. The closer I got to them the angrier I got. I heard the other chick telling her fuck me and they should've never came.

"What's up Denise?" I asked sitting in the stool next to her. The other chick rolled her eyes.

"Is there somewhere we can talk?"

"Right here is fine. As you can see no one is here but us and my manager." She rolled her eyes at Damien.

"Ugh excuse you. Don't roll your eyes at me. I didn't do anything to you. Don't get your ass beat in here." I shook my head because he was a trip.

"Let's go Denise. You don't have to tell him shit." That bitch was pissing me off in the worst way.

"Anyway, I know we aren't together anymore but I have something to tell you."

"Ok." Damien passed me a water. I took a sip as I waited for her to tell me what I'm sure I already knew. She was about to tell me when my wife, Iesha, Maria and Samantha walked in.

"Hey baby." I said and kissed her. She and the girls walked to the other end of the bar to give us privacy.

"Forget it. We can talk another time." She picked her things up to leave. I heard someone walking behind me as I waited for her to continue.

"Hi Denise. Are you here to tell my husband about his son or are you going to continue with the secret?" Her sister's mouth dropped open at the same time her's did. We sat there waiting for her answer but when she didn't my wife went in on her.

"Oh you thought we didn't know. You assumed I would be mad finding out that information but I'm the one that told him. The day you were being smart and friend requested me on Facebook told me you wanted him to know. If you didn't you would've kept quiet about it."

"You didn't tell me that." Her sister said standing there looking dumbfounded.

"This is what's about to happen. You had your fun with my husband but you can bet your life that he won't ever sleep with you again so if that was your reasoning for telling him you can cancel it. Second, we will be at LabCorp bright and early tomorrow morning and we expect to see you and your son there to have a DNA test done. You don't have to tell him what's going on until the results come back. When they come back and if he is the father, then and only then will we start making arrangements for my kids to meet him and not a minute sooner.

Your son will be well taken care of but if you run to the courts trying to get more that I am offering then we are going to have a problem. I say that because I am his wife and will be the one direct depositing the money in your account. Oh, last but not least he WILL NOT and I repeat WILL NOT be paying any of your bills or taking care of you. If you can't pay your bills or fall on hard times we will gladly take care of him until you get on your feet. Now any questions?"

"Who the fuck do you think you are bitch? I didn't have a baby by you. If you think for one minute you're going to dictate how this is going to go you have another thing coming." I moved my wife behind me and stood up and moved closer to her.

"Oh you done fucked up now talking to the Mrs. Like that." I heard Damien say behind me laughing. I grabbed her by her neck and threw her up against the wall.

"If you ever disrespect my wife like that again that will be the end of your life. If for some reason you threaten my wife, play on her phone or do any childish and petty shit to her I will end your life. If that is my son and you try and keep him from me I will end your life. Do I make myself clear?" I saw the tears running down her face. Her sister tried to pull me off but Iesha handled that shit with the quickness.

"Cream how could you put your hands on me for her?" She screamed out.

"Easy bitch. I'm his wife. I'm who you want to be but will never be. You should've stayed away like you had been doing. But believe me when I say I'm coming for you when I drop this load." I saw the shock on her face.

"Really James. Is that even your baby?" I went to get up and I felt my brother holding me back. CiCi walked right up to her and punched her in the mouth. This bitch had the nerve to swing back. Iesha, Maria, Samantha and even Damien had both of them on the ground beating the shit out of them. Louis had to get Damien up because gay or not he was still a man. When they left the girls and Damien sat at the bar laughing about what happened.

"Baby, lets go." CiCi came in my office and grabbed my hand. I locked up and followed behind her.

"Where are we going?" I saw her going in the direction of Denise's house and I got a bad feeling about what was about to happen. Especially; with my brother, Iesha and everyone else following behind us. We pulled in behind Denise and she was taking the little boy out the car. She had a nervous look on her face.

"Mommy is that my dad?" You heard him ask.

"Come here honey." CiCi said and he came over to her.

"What's your name? Your mom didn't get a chance to tell us."

"Cream Thomas but everyone calls me C.J. for short."
We all stood there in shock. Not only was I unaware he
existed; she named him after my street name. How stupid
could she be?

"How do you know that's your dad?"

"My mommy shows me pictures of him all the time.
She said that he was away and coming back home to live with
us soon." CiCi turned around and gave me the look of death. I
put my hands up and shook my head. I don't know what his
mom was telling him but I know I never told her any shit like
that.

"We came over to pick you up for a sleep over. How
does that sound?"

"Like fun. Can I go mom?" CiCi and I both gave her a
look daring her to say no. She shook her head yes. We watched
her go inside with him and a few minutes later he came back
out with a book bag and that same game controller. Luckily, I
had a game system at home in my man cave.

"Go stand by your uncle Darius and uncle Louis. We
have to talk to your mom real quick."

"Wow I have uncles? Do I have any cousins, sisters or brothers?" We heard him asking when he got to them.

"You can't just come by here demanding my son come with you? And what happened to them not meeting your other kids until you knew for sure." She had the nerve to say.

"We came by to see him for ourselves but he looks just like me and my other son Denise. What the fuck were you thinking not telling me I had a kid?"

"You said you didn't want any kids and that only your wife would have them."

"Exactly. If you knew that why did you keep the baby? Better yet you should've just told me once you had him."

"I came to the club but you were so far up her ass you ignored me. It was the right thing to do."

"The right thing to do. Do you see how happy he is to see his father? You kept him away for your own selfish reasons. The only reason you came out with it is because my wife figured it out. You better hope I bring him back and I dare you to call the cops. I'm sure the courts would get a kick out of you keeping him away."

159

"Fine. Let me know when you're dropping him off."

"I sure will." CiCi responded.

"I wasn't talking to you."

"Doesn't matter. My husband will never be the one to drop him off so don't expect to get your panties wet thinking about it. Oh, if I find out you on some sneaky shit I'm whooping your ass." The drive to my mom's house was quiet. We knew he was my son but I still wanted to take the test. When we walked through the door Summer and Lyric were the first ones to open their mouths.

"Who is this and why does he look like my cousin Junior?" Everyone laughed and walked away. I didn't find shit funny but evidently everyone else did.

"Who looks like me?" Junior asked walking in the room and stopping short when he saw C.J. I had all the kids come in the living room to explain what was going on. It took a while to get them to understand because all they knew were CiCi and I. They didn't understand how he had a different mommy but Junior and Patience didn't. I couldn't use Lyric's situation because she thought Iesha was her mom. They planned on telling her the truth when she got older but for now that's all she knew.

"Daddy didn't know about C.J. and neither did I but guess what now you have a big brother that you can play with." CiCi told Junior who wasn't having it.

"Well he's not sleeping in my room or touching my toys." Junior told him.

"I have my own toys and I don't want to sleep in your room. I have my own room anyway." I saw this shit going differently in my head. Who knew kids this young would act like this.

"Who you talking to like that?" Summer asked and now all three of them were surrounding C.J.

"It's about to go down at the playground, ya know." Louis said mimicking the song by the group ABC.

"Get your little asses in here right now. All four of you." I heard my mom yell out. She let their ass have it and made each of them apologize and hug.

"Ok then. Lets get them home." CiCi said getting all three of them ready. The next day I helped my wife get the kids up and sat them down at the table for breakfast.

"CiCi, do you love my daddy?" C.J. asked out of the blue

"Yes. Why do you ask?"

"Because my mom said he was coming home to be with us but you and him have a house together and he lives here."

"C.J. I'm not sure why your mom told you that but I didn't even know about you. CiCi is your step mom and I'm not leaving her for anyone. I know you may want to see your mom and I together because that's what you were told but its not going to happen." I made sure I was very clear when I told him that.

"Ok. CiCi I like you as my stepmom so far. Do you think I can stay on the weekends?"

"You can stay whenever you want. This is your second house and we are your extended family." The way CiCi accepted my son made me fall in love with her even more. I know he was before her time but she still could've walked away and didn't. This was just another speed bump we got

over. I wasn't letting anything, or anyone destroy what my

wife and I had, and I meant it.

Tasha

It's been a while since I heard from Monster, so I just wrote his ass off. Malcolm and I came up with a great plan to get Cream to leave CiCi. Who knew his sneaky ass was that obsessed over her and slipped something in her drink? I know he wanted her back but damn a man has to be real desperate to do some shit like that.

When he came back and told me they slept together, and he recorded it I told him to hold on to it. I knew Cream wasn't going to allow someone to get in between their relationship. That video was the perfect thing to use against her later.

I also found out that Iesha and that nigga Darius finally got married. I tried to get inside but the shit was locked down like they were on an army base. If you weren't on the list there was no way of entering. I even tried to get in through the staff entrance and they were on it. They came back from their two-week honeymoon not too long ago and seem to be living like newlyweds but I'm about to shut that shit down. I had a plan in the works to finally get rid of her. I don't know why I was thinking about that shit while he was digging in my guts.

"Fuck, I'm about to cum." I moaned out as he fucked me from the back.

"Well, let it go then." He whispered in my ear. I thought Monster had a big dick and his sex game was good but this nigga Malcolm shit was on point. Yup, I'm fucking him now since Monster is MIA. He doesn't know that CiCi is my daughter and for now I'm going to keep it that way.

"Damn Malcolm what you trying to do? Get me strung on that dick?" He grinned and got up and went to the bathroom.

"I'm ready to get CiCi back." He said walking out. I can admit I was a tad bit hurt that he brought that up right after we had sex.

"Give me your phone." He handed it to me and I went to his videos to find the one of him and CiCi. This nigga was definitely obsessed. He had photos of her going in and out of stores, the night of Iesha's bachelorette party and even some of her at the house with her kids and Cream.

I found the video of them and hit send to her phone I saw the sex video, but he was raping her and you can tell she was out of it. I sent a message that read *"If you don't meet me at the same house we had sex at, I'm sending this to your husband."* It didn't take long for her to respond.

CiCi: *Why are you doing this to me?*

Malcolm: *Because I want you. You're never going to be happy unless it's with me.*

CiCi: *Malcolm, this is crazy. What you did to me was foul and I will never speak to you again.*

Malcolm: *You should've never left and I wouldn't have needed to slip that in your drink. I have to admit that was some of the best sex I ever had.*

CiCi: *Goodbye and don't text my phone again.*

Malcolm: *You have two hours to get there.*

CiCi: *I can't. My husband is not going to let me out of his sight.*

Malcolm: *Find a way or he gets this video.*

I got a kick out of sending those messages to her. I could tell she was nervous and didn't want her husband to see

166

it. Malcolm had the biggest smile on his face when he glanced over the text. He and I discussed meeting up later and said our goodbyes. Little did he know I was going to show up at the same time? I ran to my little apartment to change and got ready to watch the fireworks.

Two hours came and I was already outside waiting for her to show up. She stepped out the car and I immediately got jealous. CiCi didn't look like she had suffered from anything I did to her. I don't want say it but my daughter was a BAD BITCH in all ways. She had security behind her car but she put her hand up to tell them to wait in the truck.

"What do you want Malcolm?" I heard when I snuck in the back door.

"Do you want something to drink?" *He had to be the dumbest motherfucker I knew. Who ask a person they drugged if they wanted another drink?*

"Hell no. I just came here to ask you to delete the video and leave me alone. My husband doesn't need to see that."

"Fuck him CiCi. He hurt you and yet you found it in your heart to go back to him."

"Ok he cheated and I took him back; that's my business. But you drugged and raped me. What you did is ten times worse? You are lucky I haven't told my husband what you did yet because when he finds out you're a dead man walking." She was confident as she spoke.

"I'm not deleting shit and I dare you to walk out that door." She had her hand on the doorknob.

"Or what? What are you going to do? Send him the video. Fuck it, send it. I can't have you blackmailing me over something that will never happen again."

"What's his number?" I couldn't stand it anymore. I had to walk in because this idiot was fucking up everything.

"Give me the phone. I'll send it." I said walking in the room surprising the hell out of her. She came charging at me but I pulled my gun out and pointed it straight at her. He handed me the phone and I sent the video to Cream's phone. Yes, I had all of their numbers. I was just waiting to use them and this seems like the perfect time to use his.

"Hello CiCi." She gave me the death stare.

"Hello mother."

"MOTHER? What the fuck Tasha?"

"Let me guess you didn't know and you've been fucking her."

"No he didn't and yes he has. I must say daughter you have these men going crazy over you. But I can say one thing about you and Iesha."

"What?"

"You two picked some men with big dicks and a great sex game. However, I haven't had Cream or Darius yet. I guess you're keeping them to yourselves." She came walking closer and I cocked the gun back. She put her hands up in a surrender stance. Her phone started ringing, which let me know the games were about to begin.

"Put that shit on speaker." I told her. She didn't want to answer it and that told me it was Cream.

"No." I pushed the gun into her temple.

"Now. Like I said. Put that shit on speaker."

"Hello."

"Hey baby. Where are you? We need to talk." I was shocked at how calm he was.

"I'm on my way home. And yes we do."

"Ok I'll see you soon." They said their goodbyes and hung up.

"Yo, I don't know what the fuck is going on but I'm out of here."

"Oh Malcolm don't leave yet. Can't you see you're about to be a father?" He stopped in his tracks and turned around smiling. I saw the tears rolling down CiCi's face and that shit had me laughing. I could tell by how big her stomach was that it had to be Cream's baby but this nigga so stupid he couldn't see it. He did that shit to her two months ago and by the looks of it she had to be at least four if not more.

"I'm about to be a dad CiCi."

"Malcolm this is not your baby."

"It has to be. You and your husband haven't been together." Just as he said that you could hear someone banging at the door. I could tell she felt a little relieved. I forgot she had security waiting for her. I kept my gun pointed at her as Malcolm and I walked backwards out the door. I saw a red light on my shirt and knew it was a laser. Fuck it, if I'm about to die so is she. I started shooting until there were no more bullets in my gun.

I felt someone pick me up off the ground and drag me to the car. I thought I was dead for a second but God was on my side. He must not want me dead yet because this is the second time I escaped death. We pulled up at my apartment and that's when I realized I was hit.

There was blood pouring out my leg and arm. When Malcolm noticed he made me stay in the car and started driving. When we stopped we were at some hospital that he told me took us forty-five minutes to get to. We got inside and they remove the two tourniquets he had on me and took me to surgery. I couldn't wait to get out and wreak more havoc.

Cream

Two weeks ago I found out through DNA that I had another son. Yes, Cream Junior was mine biologically. It pissed me off that Denise's stupid ass would keep him away from me that long over some petty shit. No, I won't even think twice about saying I understand why she did it because there was no excuse. My son has been living in the same town as me and I didn't know. I don't ever want my wife out in the streets fighting but I think I want her to whoop her ass when she drops my daughter. Yes, we found out we were having another girl.

Today, I had to run to the club to pick up some paperwork and tonight was the night we were going to take the girls to the building and surprise them. We were supposed to take them the same day the CO went through but as you can see that didn't happen. I was talking to Damien when my phone rang from one of the security guys guarding my wife.

"Hey boss. Your wife has us over here at the same address where she had that consultation. You told us to contact you if she returns."

"Good looking out. Send me the address and keep a eye out on her." We hung the phone up and I called her on her cell and told her we needed to talk. The way her voice sounded made me think something was wrong.

After I hung up, I realized I had a text message. When I opened it up, my mouth hit the floor. I was sitting here watching some man fucking my wife. I ran downstairs and hopped in my car headed to the destination the security sent me. By the time I got there you could hear sirens in the distance and one of the security guys was carrying CiCi out in his arms.

"What the fuck happened?"

"Baby, we really need to talk." She said going in and out of consciousness. I handed my keys to one of the other guys and told them to take our vehicles home. I didn't realize she was bleeding until the doctor asked me if she had been shot. I looked down and she had blood on her clothes but I don't know where it came from.

"I don't know. Please don't let her die."

"Who are you to her?"

"I'm her husband. Whatever she needs give it to her. A transfusion, anything, just make sure she doesn't die." Once she was in the back and I made all the necessary phone calls I asked the guy to tell me exactly what went down. He told me after he sent me the address he heard yelling coming from the house. He and the other guys banged on the door and when they didn't answer one of them kicked it down. He said it was a man and another woman in there and that she started shooting. By the time they got around the house both of them were gone.

He described to me what both of them looked like and the guys description was the same of who was in the video. He passed me CiCi's phone and I began going through her messages and after reading them that's when it hit me who Malcolm was.

This was that same nigga when we first got together she went to dinner with and my ex jumped her in the bathroom. Then he called her and when I spoke to him and shut shit down he hung up. How the fuck did they hook back up. If she has been with him the entire time I'm killing both of them. I made a call to Louis and told him I want all hospitals checked for gunshot victims in the area and that I would pay good money to the person if they kept her there. He told me the female was hit more than once but I still couldn't figure out who she was.

"What happened to her? Is she ok?" Iesha and Maria both bombarded me with questions.

"I don't know. When I got there they were bringing her to truck. I didn't even know she was hit until we got here." Over the next twenty minutes everyone was there in the waiting room. I feel like I just can't catch a break when it comes to us. The doctor came out hours later to tell us what was going on.

"Hi Mr. Thomas. I'm Dr. Miller and I wanted to update you on your wife's status." We shook hands and I walked him over to where everyone else was. There was no need for me to repeat what he was about to say.

"You're wife and baby are doing just fine. She was shot in her shoulder, which the bullet went straight through and came out the back and in the leg. She has a cast on her leg and her arm is in a sling. We couldn't give her any narcotics due to the baby so she will be in a lot of pain. The most we could give her was Tylenol and hopefully that will allow some of the pain to subside. They are moving her to a room as we speak and the nurse will be down to get you when they're done." I shook his hand and waited for the nurse to come get us.

"Why does mommy keep getting hurt?" Junior asked lying in bed with her. She had been home now for three days and was just starting to feel a little better.

"Mommy ended up seeing grandma again and you know what happens when I see her."

"I know. She is mean to you. When I get older I'm going to kill her myself for you." I had to laugh because he was definitely my son. I told him to go downstairs with the other kids to watch TV.

"CiCi, what's really going on?" She turned her head and I saw a few tears coming down her face.

"Whatever it is you have to trust that your husband will handle it." I turned her face to me and kissed her lips.

"Cream I would never cheat on you. I thought you would know that but when you assumed I did you made me feel like you had no faith in me and that your trust in me was gone." I sat on the bed and listened to her talk because it wasn't much I could say. I did accuse her without finding out the truth.

"When I first found out you cheated on me with the detective I ran to Malcolm." My face got tight when she said that. I knew at that moment what was coming next.

"I found comfort in him and yes we did sleep together. I told you I wasn't with anyone because you and I were separated and I didn't want any problems. After, you and I got back on track I stopped all contact with him. Recently, he got my email address somehow and asked me to do a consultation. Of course, I didn't know it was him at first. I was wondering why it didn't go through you and instead of asking you I went on the call. I fell in love with the house when I got there and couldn't wait to decorate."

"Why didn't you tell me you were there?"

"I didn't think I would be that long. When he opened the door I stepped back and yelled at him for setting the whole thing up. He asked me to come in to talk and I should've just left but I was trying to be nice. I get inside and he has a candlelight dinner set up." I could feel myself getting angry because I knew she slept with him from the video I got but I needed to know why. She was hesitant to discuss the next part so I laid in the bed with her and let her know it was fine.

"I took a sip of water and listen to him tell me he wanted me back and so forth. My mouth started to get dry so I drank more water." She didn't have to tell me anymore because I already knew what happened but she wanted to finish.

"I went to the bathroom and threw water on my face. I felt tired, dizzy and I was feeling weird. James that's all I remember. I woke up naked and you were ringing my phone off the hook. I wanted to tell you but I was ashamed for even putting myself in a situation like that. I should've just told you." She was crying hysterical.

"Why were you there today?"

"He sent me a text message threatening to send the video to you. James, I don't care if I hated you I would never want you to see me having sex with another man. I got there and asked him to erase the video and leave me alone and then

178

my mother stepped out. Do you know she was sleeping with Malcolm and Monster? Neither one knew she was my mother and the look on Malcolm's face when he found out was priceless."

"He's dead and so is your mom."

"James, he thinks the baby is his." I sat up and looked at her.

"My mother told him that. You know this is your baby right?"

"Without a doubt." I knew for a fact that was my baby. She was too far along for it to be anyone else's. Even if she carrying someone else's it would still be mine. I'm the only man to be her husband or kids father. Say what you want but it is what it is.

"I'm having a hard time locating your mom because we don't know what she looks like. Darius, snapped some photos of her in the store but they were blurry."

"I have one." I gave her a shocked look.

"Once she came in the house and started talking to Malcolm I snatched my phone out and snapped a few photos.

Hand me my phone." I gave it to her and she showed it to me and the woman I saw was not her mother. Whoever did her surgery should receive a medal because you would never guess it was her.

"Baby, I'm sorry I didn't give you the chance to explain yourself and accused you of cheating. I should've known better. I also apologize for acting out and sleeping with another woman."

"I can't be mad because we were separated. But at least you found your son and that's all that matters."

"You mean you found him. I still didn't know because she never had him around which I can understand that too. I wasn't ready to meet her kid anyway. Who knew he was mine?" I stayed in the house with my wife until she fell asleep.

I sent the photos to Louis, Darius, all the girls and the security teams to show them what Tasha Barnes looked like and I wanted her found and brought to me alive. I received confirmed texts from every one and now I was on my way to my next destination.

I must say this nigga had a nice place. Too bad he fucked with the wrong one and he won't be living in it long. Everyone knows I don't fuck around when it comes to my family so to hear he did this shit to my wife and was in cahoots with her mom he had to go. I heard a car door close and the key turning in the lock. I sat in the dark waiting for him to realize I was there. He must've been stupid because I would be extra careful after the shit they pulled. He was taking to long so I let my presence be known and he damn near shitted on himself.

"Hello Malcolm."

"Who are you?" He couldn't see me because I hadn't turned the light on yet. But when I did his eyes almost popped out of his head.

"Do you know who I am now?" He stood there stuck. I knew this dude was scary but damn.

"I didn't shoot her." I stood up wiping my jeans and fixing my clothes.

"No, but you slipped a drug in her drink and raped her."

"It wasn't like that."

"It wasn't like that huh? Is that why you think the baby is yours?" He stood in the same spot.

"Her mother told me it was mine."

"All you had to do was look at her stomach and see that it wasn't. But that also tells me that not only did you rape her but you fucked her without a condom. You see Malcolm that's my pussy and I told you that when you called her phone some years back trying to get a date with her." I saw the shock on his face.

"Yea a nigga remembers who you are."

"I just wanted her to be with me. You're no good for her."

"And you are? A man that feels he has to drug someone to sleep with them and then videotape her without knowing. Oh, by the way that may have been the best pussy you ever got but it will be your last. Now that I think about it; I watched the video and she was just lying there so how could you say that? It doesn't even matter because you won't be able to tell anyone about it."

"What do you want from me? Just don't kill me."

"Give me the password to your phone and Tasha's phone number. Matter of fact where is she?"

"I'm not giving you shit."

"Oh you tough now? Lets see how tough you are when I beat that ass." I hit him and he was out for the count. I continued beating him so bad I heard the crack in his jaw and nose. I kicked and stomped on him until it looked like one of his eyes popped out. I was done playing with his ass. I checked his pockets and found his phone.

"This is for my wife." I emptied my clip in his head and walked out.

Today I was waiting for a call from someone that told me he ran into CiCi's mom. Actually he was fucking her. She stayed sleeping with these young dudes but hey whatever floats their boat. As long as he came through with the information I didn't care what he did with her.

Next up Tasha Barnes

CiCi

I was glad I told my husband what really happened; it was weighing heavy on me. I should've told him sooner but I was being childish and let him think what he wanted but now look. I know he killed Malcolm because it's been a month and I haven't heard anything from him. James and I were back to being a family but he wasn't himself. Something was going on with him. He seemed stressed out all the time and anytime I asked if he was ok he would just shake his head. I just came form the doctor and he took the cast off but told me I needed to take it easy. He tried to set me up with physical therapy but I wasn't having that.

I was six months pregnant and I was horny as hell. It was after nine and all the kids were asleep. I text James to see where he was and instead of him answering he walked in the bedroom and straight to the shower. I picked his clothes up and I saw specks of blood on them. Then it came to me. He must've been tearing the city up looking for my mom and it was stressing him out. I stripped out my pajamas and laid back on the bed. I was so horny I started rubbing on my clit when I felt his tongue take over. It wasn't even thirty seconds later when I erupted down his face.

"Damn baby, you needed that." He said after I came a few more times. I sat up in the bed and pulled him close to me where my face was eye level with my best friend. I took my hands and gently stroked and sucked on him.

I spit on the tip just the way he liked and ran my tongue in the slit. He moaned out a little. I sucked the life out of his dick. His legs started getting weak so he sat back on the bed. I got on my knees and continued satisfying him.

"Ahhh damn CiCi. You have the best pussy and give me the best head. Shit, you are everything I need in a woman."

"I know." I said and straddled his lap to bring him back to life. Once I felt him stiffen underneath me I put him inside and hitched a ride on his pony.

"Baby, I'm cumming. Don't stop." I yelled out as he pounded in and out from the back.

"Cum on your dick then." I swear every time I came it felt like water running out of me.

"Make your husband cum." He said and I started throwing my ass back and making it clap at the same time.

"Oh shit. Oh shit. Fuckkkkkk CiCi." I felt him shoot everything he had in me. I turned around and kissed him aggressively. I was so in love with him and couldn't get enough.

"Does my baby want some more?" He asked and I nodded my head yes.

"Then tell me."

"I want you to make love to me James as only you can." He laid me down on the bed gently and did exactly what I asked him. The way he had me moaning and how he had me feeling was like no other. I know he slept with that other chick but I hoped and prayed he didn't give himself to her the way he did me.

"I'm not cheating on you Ci." I glanced up at him because I didn't know where that came from.

"I never said you were."

"I know but I know my wife too. I see the way you stare at me when I come home late or when I give you short

186

answers. I'm out here looking for your mom and it requires me to be on my shit."

"I believe you."

"Good. I'm not about to allow anyone to destroy our marriage anymore."

"Can I ask you something?" I wasn't sure if I should ask because I didn't know if I wanted the answer.

"Yea babe."

"Did you make love to her the way you make love to me?"

"Why do you do that to yourself?"

"I ask because it tells me how you felt about her. I guess it's a woman's thing."

"No I didn't. Yes, I slept with her but like I told you before I will never give my all to a woman unless its you."

"Did you go down on her?"

"That would be giving her my all, so no. CiCi, you don't have to try and compare your sex to another female. No woman will feel the same that I sleep with just like no man will feel the same you sleep with. All I can say to you is, you have the best pussy I ever had in my life. The blowjobs you give me are out of this world and I'm not just saying that because you're my wife. I've been telling you that since the first time we had sex. No one will ever compare to you no matter how many tricks she has up her sleeve."

"Really." I smiled listening to him.

"Yes. It's like having a favorite food. No matter how many people try and duplicate it, it won't top your favorite. Baby, you're all I need and I don't ever want you second guessing yourself."

****

The next day he wanted me to go down to some building with him and my sister and Darius was supposed to meet us there. It looked like an empty building when you first look at it. I saw some construction people at the top with a sign to hand but I didn't see what it said. When we got inside the place was huge. Then we walked next door and that place was even bigger.

"Ok. What is this place and why are we here?" When Darius told us what is was for Iesha and I jumped up and down and started screaming. We were already talking about what we were going to get, who we would hire and the list went on and on. Darius walked up behind my sister and kissed the back of her neck. I turned around and Cream was standing in the corner looking out the window. I went over to where he was and wrapped my arms around his waist the best I could. My stomach was poking out a lot now.

"Are you ok?" I asked and he turned around to face me. He lifted my chin and placed kisses on my lips, cheeks, nose and forehead. I was wearing some stretch pants and his nasty ass put his hands in my pants and brought me to an orgasm right there. I thought we were bad but when I heard my sister and Darius in the other room moaning I knew we weren't. I unzipped his pants and got down on my knees bringing him to his own orgasm. I stood up just as they came out the back.

"I love you Mrs. Thomas." He said kissing my lips allowing us both to taste one another.

"I love you too Mr. Thomas." He turned me around and stood me in front of him.

189

"You know we're finishing this later." I just shook my head. I know people think we have a lot of sex and we do. But we're still young and having fun. It's only right. The guys to us out to dinner and we discussed when the grand opening would be. My life was finally going well but I know it won't last too long with my mother out there lurking.

Denise

I was sitting in my house waiting for Cream's wife to drop my son off. Now that the results came back and they knew for sure he was his she made sure he was at their house every weekend. I didn't mind because I kept him away for so many years he needed to get to know him.

I may not like that bitch but she keeps my son laced in new shit and takes very good care of him. That's all he talks about when he comes back. She wasn't lying either when she said Cream would never drop him off and she was only giving the minimum amount for him. Three thousand dollars a month was ok with me; shit, I wasn't getting anything for five years.

She pulled up in a brand new BMW truck and got out to give my son a kiss. I hated the relationship they had. It was like he forgot all about me when he got around them. Yes, I hated on her. He was supposed to be mine before he was hers. I don't know what she had that locked him down right away. I do know that I miss his dick game.

Cream may not have gone down on me or even made love to me but the way he fucked had a bitch fiending for it. I masturbated plenty of times to the memories of us going at it like animals. But I know no matter how many times he had sex with me he would never love me the way he loved her. He told me from the very beginning no other woman would ever come before her whether they were together or not. I found that odd but hey if that's how he wanted it.

"Hey mommy." I heard taking me out my thoughts.

"Hey son. Did you have fun?"

"Yea. Me, Junior, Summer and Lyric were going to beat up these two boys at the playground." I laughed because the first day they met him they didn't like him and now they are thick as thieves. Junior has even had his mom call over here just so they could talk on the phone. He and I talked a little more and I put him to bed. My sister stopped by and asked if I wanted to go out. I couldn't because my son was home but she brought her teenage babysitter with her to watch her son at my house too.

Two hours later we were headed to the club Cream and his brother owned. Don't ask me why but I felt like my sister had something up her sleeve. We weren't there long when Cream and the other guy Louis walked in. I swear Cream could get my panties wet just looking at me. He spoke to both of us and walked upstairs to his office. My sister followed behind his friend and I went behind him. Call me a groupie but if you had a piece of Cream you would understand.

"How the fuck did you get up here?" He stood up walking towards me.

"It doesn't matter. I just want some dick and I promise I'll leave." He grinned and shook his head. I started taking my shirt off and walked closer to him when his wife stepped out the bathroom and hit me so hard I was almost back at the door.

"Bitch, are you crazy trying to fuck my husband?"

"Nah. You know how good that dick is. I would be a fool not to try to get it again." I was going to keep fucking with her because she was pregnant. I knew it wasn't much she could do.

"I definitely do. And that dick that you so desperately want belongs to me and only me. That's why he won't fuck with that garbage you have in between your legs."

"It wasn't garbage when he was fucking me."

"Boo you were just something to do until his wife took him back. You are the second bitch that swore her pussy was golden and that he couldn't live without it. I'm here to tell you if there's one he can't live without its mine. Aint that right baby?" When he said yes I was fuming.

"Really Cream. What was all that my shit you were talking that my shit was tight and good?" I said throwing it in her face.

"It was at the time. But my wife's pussy has me sprung. She by far has the best pussy in the world. No other woman will ever compare to what she has. Yes, I fucked you and took you out of town but you were never my main chick. This woman right here is the only for me." I was so mad I picked up a wine bottle that was on the shelf and threw it in their direction. The shit almost hit her and I was happy but I couldn't get out the office fast enough. He had me by the back of my neck with a gun to my head.

"Don't shoot. I'm pregnant."

"I don't give a fuck. I told you I would end you if you did anything to my wife." I heard the gun cock.

"It's your baby Cream." The minute I said that he dropped me to the ground and turned around to look at his wife. I saw the tears running down her face as she shook her head. I was more than satisfied that I hurt her. Now all I had to do was get the fuck out of there before he remembered I made his wife cry and kill me anyway. I picked my shirt and phone up off the floor and ran out the door. I snatched my sister up who was laughing in Louis face. I hate to tell her but he was just as faithful as Darius and Cream. She wasn't getting anything from him.

"Bitch. I told Cream I was pregnant." I yelled out after we got in the car.

"Oh shit. What happened?"

"He was about to shoot me. I had to say something."

"Are you pregnant?"

"Yea. I just don't know by who though." We both busted out laughing and drove back to my house. The babysitter was sleep so she stayed in the extra bedroom. I laid on my bed still laughing at how bad I hurt her. That's what the fuck she gets for thinking her shit don't stink. I'm sure I'll have to deal with the repercussions of it tomorrow but for now I'm going to enjoy the moment.

Cream

I swear I can't win for losing. Every time I get back on track with my wife some otter shit pops up. CiCi came to the club with me to hang out with Damien. I went to meet Louis outside to discuss this shit with my mother in law. I didn't want to take any chances of anyone hearing us. Anyway, I come back and she was in the bathroom with the door open stripping for me.

Unfortunately, this dumb bitch comes in trying to fuck. I grinned because I knew my wife was about to get in her ass. The shit was funny until the bottle almost hit CiCi. All I saw was red after that.

The moment I cocked the gun back and she said the baby was mine, I looked at my wife and the tears were already flowing. I didn't know if she was lying but I couldn't kill her and she was pregnant with my baby. The look on my wife's face was pure disgust. All the shit we been through and I fucked around and got another woman pregnant. I don't know what I was thinking. I remember the exact day I slept with her unprotected.

We were driving to Maryland for me to check on some shipments coming in. I told Denise we were going on vacation. I did take her to the Inner Harbor in Baltimore but that wasn't shit compared to all the times I traveled the world with my wife. I would've never brought my wife with me on a trip like this but hey this chick wanted to be up under me so it is what it is.

We went to the Hard Rock Cafe to eat and I was throwing back shots. I was there with her but my mind was on CiCi and drinking was easing my pain. We got back to the hotel and my dick was in her mouth the second the door closed. After I came, she got me hard again and not thinking I stuck my dick in her with no condom. I didn't remember everything but I know we had sex a few times that night.

When I looked in the garbage the next day, I didn't see any wrappers or the box the condoms came in. I knew I fucked up then but I pushed it to the back of my mind. I came home and went straight to the doctors and was tested for everything. *This was the second time I did my wife like that. I started*

thinking maybe I wasn't ready to be married but I did know no
other man was going to be with CiCi.

The doctors' office contacted me a couple of weeks later and cleared me of anything. Thank goodness for that but now I'm sitting here looking stupid with a possible baby on the way. My wife ran out of here and Denise was no longer in the bar. I hopped in my car and sped to Denise house and started banging on the door.

"Why are you banging on the door like that?" Her sister asked with an attitude.

"Move bitch." I pushed her ass to the side and took the steps two at a time. I snatched her out the bed by her neck.

"Cream stop. I'm pregnant. You're going to kill the baby." I felt myself squeezing her tighter each time she spoke. Her face was turning blue and I think she peed on herself. I gave zero fucks at this point and planned on watching her die. My phone started vibrating and it was my mom. I answered the phone while I still had her ass in the air.

"What's up ma?" I never took my eyes off her. I wanted to see her soul leave her body.

"What is going on and why is CiCi hysterical crying?" I felt myself loosening up.

"Where is she?" I needed to hear my wife's voice in order to calm down. That was the only person besides my mom that could get to me when I was this mad.

"James whatever you did, you have to make it right with your wife. She is at the hospital in labor."

"She's only seven and a half months. It's too early."

"Well the baby is ready to come so get your ass here."

"I'll be back." I dropped her to the floor and she looked dead. I lifted her by the shirt and whispered in her ear.

"You can kill yourself for all I care but if you try and sneak off with my son I will find you and kill you. I won't care who the fuck baby you're carrying. Someone will be watching you." I stepped over her and ran down the steps.

"Was that necessary?" Her sister asked.

"You know you got a smart ass mouth. I'm sure you know what she did. You two can think it's cute all you want but we'll see how cute it is when you're taking a dirt bath on the side of her." I saw fear written all over her face.

"Yea. Don't stop talking shit now."

"But she's pregnant."

"And she's not my wife and I don't know for sure if that's my baby. Her best bet right now is to get rid of it. She has the money to do it because she gets a nice chunk of change in her bank account every month. Since you talked her into coming to the club so you can hit on my boy you need to talk her into doing that or it's going to be nothing but problems for both of you."

"I don't have anything to do with that."

"The minute you cosigned that shit, you put yourself in it." I left out the house and rushed over to the hospital. When I got there, they already had her prepped for delivery.

Iesha was on one side and my mom swapped with me so I could be on the other. I kissed her lips and grabbed her hand. A few hours later she pushed my daughter Sienna Thomas into the world weighing at eight pounds and ten ounces. She didn't want her to have a middle name; saying one name was enough for her. The nurses took her to the NICU to check her out.

They brought Sienna back in and told us she was fine. Her lungs were developed, all her vitals were good and she was a screamer. The doctor said she was so big even though she was preemie it helped her lungs develop faster.

I looked down at my daughter and she looked just like me. Her eyes looked gray but otherwise she was all me. I laid her on my chest and we both dosed off. When I opened my eyes CiCi was feeding and talking to her. I wondered if I even deserved someone as good as her to be my wife. The lady brought in the papers to sign the birth certificate and the photo people came shortly after.

It's been a few weeks since my daughter was born and I hadn't heard a peep from Denise. My mom picked my son up every Friday and dropped him back off Sunday nights. If I went over there, I would definitely kill her.

****

"James." I heard CiCi call out.

"Yea."" I walked in the room holding Sienna in one arm and Patience was walking beside me.

"Put the kids down. We need to talk." I knew it was

coming I was just waiting for her to say it. I went back in the room to hear what she had to say.

"James you know how much I love you right?" I nodded my head.

"James, I'm not a weak bitch and the disrespect from you and your bitches are at an all-time high and I'm over it. How much longer do you think I'm supposed to deal with it?"

"CiCi no one will ever disrespect you in my presence or not. You know that. I shut that shit down right away."

"What, you think you giving away my dick isn't disrespectful and the fact those bitches can even say they had it, is a smack in the face." I ran my hand down my face waiting for whatever she was about to hit me with. I felt it coming.

"You continue to hurt me over and over and I sit back and take it. I don't want to be a woman who tries to stay in her marriage when the man acts like he doesn't." I went to say something but she wouldn't let me.

"From here on out, you'll be sleeping in the guest bedroom until we find out if that baby is yours." I remained quiet.

"James you are my heart but if that is your child, as hard as it will be, this marriage is over."

"CiCi."

"I mean what I say. As far as, if I get horny. I'll come to you." I shook my head because I wish she would lay down with another man.

"But if you even think about going outside this marriage before it's over, I promise on everything, you'll need to sleep with one eye open." I couldn't believe she was standing there threatening me.

"Now come over here and eat this pussy until I don't have any more fluids in my body."

"But you just said…" I tried to get out.

"I don't care what I said, just do it." I shook my head and went to where she was and gave her what she wanted. I wasn't about to give her head and not get my shit off. I rammed my dick in her so hard she screamed out. One of the nannies had to knock on the door to make sure she was ok. Fuck that I made sure that each time she walked she felt me.

"I love you CiCi and I'm going to get us back to where

we used to be." I kissed her forehead and left the room. My next stop was back to Denise house. I was driving her to the abortion clinic. There was no way I was losing my family.

CiCi

It was a week since I made my husband sleep in a different room and I hated to admit it, but I was missing him. It was killing me not to have him come back to our bed. He was in the house every night by five to have dinner with us and stayed in. If I text him or he missed my call, he would hit me right back. Not that he wasn't doing it before but I had his ass nervous that I was leaving.

Sometimes a woman has to put fear in that man's heart in order for him to act right. Yea we can say we have the best pussy and he's not going anywhere but that's not always true. Threaten that nigga with leaving and he'll shape up eventually; too scared you'll start sleeping with someone else.

"Let me get this right. You kicked him out the room, told him the marriage was over if that was his baby and then made him go down on you." Maria asked drinking her soda she just ordered at Red Lobster.

"Yup. And you can bet he did what the fuck I said and then some." I told them laughing.

"Are you really going to leave him?" Samantha asked. She had a sad look on her face because she loved James like her brother.

"No. But he doesn't know that. I want his ass scared. I don't want him to have any more kids unless they're by me. He was with her during out separation. I get that he slept with her; I think I'm madder he didn't strap up." They all shook their heads agreeing with what I said.

We stayed in the restaurant drinking and laughing. I felt someone staring and when I looked around it was that dumb bitch Denise and her sister. She had the nerve to give me attitude like she's not sitting there possibly with my husbands' baby in her stomach. We were about to leave so of course I had to walk over and speak.

"Hello ladies." She sucked her teeth.

"That's not nice Denise. You know I may have to be a stepmom again to your baby."

"You trying to be funny?" I had no idea what she was talking about.

"What?"

"You know your husband took me to the abortion clinic and made me get rid of it."

"I didn't know that." I was smiling inside but I was pissed he was with her and didn't mention it.

"Yea his ignorant ass came in the room and made sure they did it."

"Wait the doctor let him go in the back?" Iesha asked smirking.

"Yes. They were too scared to tell him no." We all fell out laughing. James was a piece of work.

"That's not funny." Denise said acting like she had an attitude.

"Ugh yes it is. Didn't you say he told you your pussy was good? I guess it wasn't good enough to birth any more of his kids." We went to leave and Maria reached over and knocked Denise's sister out. I mean the bitch was straight sleep on the floor. Denise jumped out her chair we all gave her a look and she went to help her sister up.

"What was that all about?" I asked once we got outside.

"That bitch was at the club that night all the shit went

down and tried to fuck Louis. She's lucky that's all I did to her." Maria hi fived Samantha.

We all pulled off, but my first stop would be to the person least expecting me. I opened the door and the two people I saw pointed upstairs. I could hear a few voices coming from the door.

"I need to speak to my husband NOW." Darius and Louis shook their head and

gave me a kiss on the cheek on their way out. The other staff rushed out of there. I shut the door behind them and walked over to James who sat there leaning back in his seat. I let my coat hit the floor, then my shirt, pants, bra and panties. The smile that came across his face and the bulge in his pants showed me he was happy to see me.

"What did I do to get this?" He ran his hands up and down my legs. I sat on his desk and spread eagle for him.

"Make me cum baby." I whispered out but loud enough for him to hear. He wasted no time making me scream his name. I wiped his mouth after he finished, got down on my knees and gave him the sloppiest head ever.

"CiCi suck all that dick. Yea, just like that. Ahhhh."
After he fed me his babies he went to work tearing my pussy
up.

"Am I off punishment yet?" He was pounding harder
and harder. I wouldn't answer so he laid me down on the desk
and spread my legs all the way. He knew how much I enjoyed
this. He put the head in and kept taking it out; teasing me.

"Please baby. I'm right there." My clit was rock hard
and about to bust.

"Not until you answer me. Am I off punishment?" As
bad as I didn't want to answer I had to. My body was waiting
to release and he was the one to do it.

"Yes James yes." He put the entire thing in and I came
so hard my body was like a fish out of water flopping on the
desk. Juices were seeping out all over like a waterfall.

"That better be the end of you putting me on
punishment. And I'm coming back in the room tonight." He
said bringing me to another one.

"This pussy so good I want to live in it. Damn baby.
Ahhhh shit. I love the fuck out of you girl." He filled me up

with more of his kids and fell on top of me. This time he listened to my heartbeat. He pulled me up and we walked in the bathroom to clean up. I stood there as he took his time washing me up. We stared into each other's eyes and I think I fell in love with him all over again.

"Why didn't you tell me you took her to get rid of the baby?" He pulled me down on his lap and kissed my neck and shoulders.

"You weren't talking to me. How did you find out?"

"She told me."

"She told you?"

"Yup. And she told us how you went in the back with the doctor."

"You damn right. I needed to hear the vacuum sucking it out. Say what you want but she could've told the doctor to say she got one and didn't. I wasn't taking any chances."

"Ok. But that may have been your baby."

"I know but if it meant losing you that was a sacrifice I had to make."

"I'm sorry you if I made you feel that way."

211

"It was my decision not yours. Don't feel bad it is what it is. She can have more kids they just won't be mine."

"You damn right." I kissed his lips and started telling him the story of how we were at the restaurant and ran into them. I also told him how Maria knocked the sister out for trying it with Louis. We both got a good laugh off of that.

A few minutes later someone knocked at the door. It was Damien telling us the few things he did with the two million dollars for turning in Monster. Even though Miguel had the drop on him they still gave Damien the money because he still made the call.

"What's for dinner tonight?" James asked while we sat there.

"I don't know. You may be sleeping in the bed again but you still have a lot of making up to do. You can start with figuring that out."

"Oh yea. I think I have just the thing to take me out of the doghouse for good." He lifted me up and grabbed my hand. After he locked his office up he led me to the car and drove me to Tiffany's in New York.

The owner opened the door because they had just closed. He took us in some room and asked us to sit tight. Some women came out and laid a black velvet cloth on the table.

"Close your eyes baby." I closed them but I was still peeking. He must've known because he got up and used his hands. My mouth was hanging open when he moved his hands. There was a diamond tennis bracelet with the anklet to match, a pair of stud earrings and a diamond necklace with a key hanging down. He turned it over and it read *C&J Forever*. You had to turn it over read because it was on the long part of the key.

"Baby, you didn't have to do this. I have enough jewelry at home."

"Yea I know but I wanted you to know you are the only one with the key to my heart."

"Here is the last thing your husband purchased for you." The man said laying a 18karat rose gold watch in front of me. I looked at the price and that shit said $7300. I told him to put it back. I don't need a watch that cost that kind of money.

James placed the watch on my wrist anyway.

"James, I know you have the money but this is crazy."

"It's ok CiCi. I'm crazy over you and you deserve nothing but the best after what you've been through. I love you so much and I'm sorry for ever hurting you."

"I know and I love you too. How am I going to top this?" Him and the people in the store laughed. I kept the watch on and he put the necklace on and had the man wrap the rest of the jewelry. We stopped at BBQ's to eat and headed back home.

Iesha

I think we were all happy that CiCi and James were back together. All the arguing and the bullshit that took place was draining everyone. I didn't say much because Darius and I pretty much went through the same thing not too long ago with Sky. I don't wish this much drama on any man and woman.

"What you daydreaming about?" Darius came in and wrapped his arms around my waist.

"Just how loving you and your brother has been a battle for CiCi and I."

"It does seem like that right."

"Seem like it. Ugh, it has been. Hopefully they can get it right this time. It took me leaving you for six months to get your shit together. He won't let her stay gone longer than a month."

"No she left him for three months remember."

"Yea, but he stayed texting her and trying to see her. He didn't leave her alone. And this last time well, we all know that didn't last long at all."

"It must be something in the Barnes genes that keep us stuck."

"You nasty as hell." I pushed him off me.

"Nasty for you baby. Lets get a quickie in before the kids get here."

"You don't know how to give quickies."

"I know so hurry up. We only have twenty minutes before they come in."

"You are a mess." I followed him upstairs and just as we were getting into it you could hear the kids downstairs yelling. I squeezed his dick with my pussy and within minutes we both exploded. Summer grown ass came bursting through the door talking shit as usual. Her and Lyric were going to be the death of me with those mouths of theirs. I told her to get in the shower and put her pajamas on and to tell Lyric to get in after her.

The twins and my other son were sitting on the couch with Darius. I told him I wanted everyone to come down to the restaurant tomorrow so we could eat there before the grand opening. I was having the chef prepare the food in buffet since I gave the waiters the night off.

Tomorrow was the grand opening of my restaurant and CiCi's interior design business grand opening was last week. She had so many people there wanting her business; she was booked for a few months already. We were both excited and decided to go by the building to make sure everything was the way we wanted it.

****

CiCi was walking in the restaurant when James, Darius, Louis and Samantha's husband came walking in with all the kids. Maria and Samantha were already there with us because Maria was partners with CiCi. Maria tried to decline but my sister wouldn't let her. Damien said he would help out when he wasn't at the bar and James was fine with that. He said he needed a break from him.

"Ok, the chef made a little bit of everything and its laid out in buffet style." I told everyone. I wanted all of us to enjoy the dinner as a family before we opened to the public. It was going to be hectic with both businesses opening and would stay that way for the first couple of months. We stayed there laughing and joking until after ten. The kids were full and worn out so we took them home.

I woke up bright and early to get my nails and hair done. The girls beat me to the shop, which was funny being that I'm usually the first one. We stayed in the shop for at least four hours. I got home and the kids were outside in the backyard with the nannies.

"Baby, let me taste it before we go out." I thought my sister and Cream were bad but he was no better. My hair was wrapped up from the shop and I had a few hours before the opening. Of course, he gave me more than just head. He and I went at it for over two hours. Thank goodness my hair stayed wrapped.

We jumped in the shower together to save time. I looked over at us and we matched each other's fly. He had on some black Versace jeans with a white shirt to match. He put on his new Balenciaga sneakers with his platinum necklace and diamond earing. I wore a black pencil skirt with a split up the side, courtesy of Versace.

I wore a white gathered sleeve top to match and some peep toe Louboutin's he just brought me. My hair was hanging down my back you know my makeup was perfect. After we gave each other the ok we kissed the kids goodbye and headed out in his Phantom. I hated this car because it was looked like in belonged in a movie from the 50's. We pulled up and the line to get in was forming already. I didn't expect people to be there already.

The grand opening was perfect. The restaurant made so much money and we later found out a few food critics were there. They gave it five stars and made it one of he best places to eat at when in the area. Things were going great for all of us but I know it's just a matter of time before my mom shows her face. I'm going to sit back and wait.

Cream

"How much longer are you going to keep me down here?" The person asked when I walked through the door. My hand connected to the persons face knocking them out instantly. For over the last three months I've been coming here and it's always the same thing.

The person would ask the question and I would fuck them up. Now that I looked at the person the sight was horrendous and I could care less. I could see the weight loss and the stench was worse. No one knew about this spot or the person but my brother and Louis. We kept it that way so we could torture the fuck out of the person.

"You want some of this cheesesteak?" Louis asked.

"How could you eat with that smell?" I had to keep my nose covered when I stepped inside he place.

"You know dam well we've smelled shit worse than this. I guess I'm used to it." He took a bite and passed me the other half of the sandwich. I closed the door, opened the window and waited for the fresh air to kick in before I ate.

"How much longer are we going to do this?" He was referring to the person we had locked up.

"It's going on what three and a half months right." He nodded his head.

"I'd say another two weeks and then we'll inform everyone else to see how they want to handle it." Just as I said that Darius walked in and started kicking the person in the stomach and face. We had to jump up and stop him. We didn't want him to kill them yet.

"I'm ready for her to die."

"I know so am I but it's not our fight. Two more weeks and I'm sure she'll be out of our lives forever." If you're wondering yes it is Tasha the girls mother that we have locked away. Three and a half months ago we got the call we were waiting for. I didn't mention it because she was receiving the same treatment she gave my wife and sister in law. The day my wife saw the blood on my clothes was the first day we found her. I almost killed her had Louis not stopped me. I try not to put my hands on a woman but if you come for my family I don't care who you are.

"Yo boss. Jarrell said she was coming to his house around nine if you want to get at her." One of my workers called and told me. Louis was with me at the time and jumped in the car with me. I didn't care that it was only six; I planned on copping a squat at his house until she showed up. I didn't want to take any chances of missing her.

"Tell Jarrell I'm on my way. I'll be parked down the street and make sure he keeps the door unlocked. I don't want to have to kick his door down." I ended the call and waited with Louis. CiCi had been texting me and I tried to get back to her but tonight I had to be on my shit. I refused to let this woman out of my sight an if my wife or Iesha couldn't kill her I sure was.

"This bitch sure is punctual, huh?" Louis asked when we saw her walk in the house. We stayed in the car for another ten minutes. I wanted to make sure she got comfortable. The door was unlocked like I instructed but no one was in the living room. You could hear moaning from the back.

"Damn, she wasted no time."

"I'm going to let her finish getting her shit off. Who am I to bust that nigga nut? He looked out so it's only fair." Louis lit a black and mild and twenty minutes later you heard the door creek.

"She's all your boss." Jarrell said and went to the bathroom. You could hear the shower turn on. I guess he wanted to wash her old ass off. Jarrell was only twenty-one and this bitch was well into her forties. I knocked on the bedroom door with my gun.

"I thought you were getting in the shower." She said lying on her stomach not bothering to turn around. I grabbed her by the hair and yanked her out the bed. When she looked in my eyes I saw fear, hurt and sadness.

"Put your fucking clothes on." I yelled at her. She had the nerve to reach out and try to grab my dick. I hit her with the butt of my gun, splitting her nose instantly.

"I'm not those weak nigga. My dick belongs to my wife only." She had this wicked laugh as she continued putting her clothes on talking shit in the process.

"Yea ok. Now you want to claim you're a saint after you cheated and almost had another baby on her." I didn't know how she got her information but it infuriated me that she was getting a kick out of the hurt CiCi went through. My fist connected to her face and I felt myself taking all my anger out on her. I had her on the ground stomping and kicking. I was ready to kill her myself. Louis had to stop and remind me it that the girls had the final say.

"Thanks man." I handed him a briefcase with a hundred thousand dollars in it.

"Boss, you didn't have to do that. You know I'll do anything for your wife and Iesha. If you don't remember this was one of the guys they saved the night Monster first came for my brother. He was shot in the stomach outside the liquor store. Yea, when he got better I put him on. His cousin was paralyzed from the waist down but he was still alive thanks to the quick thinking from the girls. I made sure all his medical bills stayed paid and that they were living like the Jones. CiCi made sure of that and she made me promise to keep him safe if he was going to be working for me.

"Take it as a bonus. And don't forget in a couple of weeks is the wedding and I better see you, Austin and your mom." I have been planning a surprise wedding for my wife.

"Come on now. You didn't even have to say that." He laughed and gave me a hug.

The day we locked Tasha up Darius and I whooped her ass a few times but made sure we had a doctor on the premises so he could nurse her back to health. We fed her bread and water and she was only allowed to shower once a week. Her hair was matted and she was in the same clothes we picked her up in. The only toilet was a bucket that sat next to her. She was allowed to empty it the same day she took a shower. I didn't care how bad it was she didn't deserve to live this long. She tortured my wife for four months and that's exactly what I was doing to her.

****

Tomorrow, I was marrying my wife again. She had no idea what we set up for her. The girls helped me with the dress and what colors she would want. There wasn't going to be any bachelor or bachelorette parties. The girls took her to New

York for the night so I could have everything set up for her when she returned. The tents were put up along with the tables and chairs. The caterer called to say she would be there around ten in the morning to set up and so did the DJ. Miguel brought the family and sent Violet to New York with the girls. Planning a wedding is too much work; now I see why women say that's the most stressful moment in their life after giving birth. Thank goodness I had help because justice of the peace was sounding real good right now.

"You ready son." CiCi's dad asked me. We were picking our suits up. C.J and Junior were in the back listening to their beats.

"Yup. I have been ready. That's the only woman for me."

"Good. You two were made for each other." All of us stayed up all night laughing, drinking and smoking. I was taking a shower when I could hear my phone ringing. I knew it was CiCi because no one else was calling me this late.

"What's up baby?" I called her when I got out the shower.

"I miss you James. I want to come home but they won't let me." She was whining on the phone.

"Baby, you'll be home in a few hours. Just enjoy yourself."

"They're all drunk and fell asleep on me." I laughed and shook my head.

"Baby, can you make me cum over the phone?" My wife was a freak and I loved every minute of it. After we had phone sex she wanted to stay on the phone with me until she fell asleep.

"CiCi you are spoiled you know that right?"

"You did it." I couldn't do shit but smile. She was right I spoiled the shit out of her and that's why she didn't want for anything. I may have done my dirt but she always remained first.

"I love you James."

"I love you too baby. Keep the phone by your ear. I'm going to sleep but I won't hang up."

"Ok baby." I heard her say barely. I knew she was falling asleep. I felt like we were two teenagers.

CiCi

It was nine in the morning and these fools were still asleep. It was Saturday and I was ready to get back to my kids and husband. I thought about him saying I was spoiled and he was right. I couldn't get a good night sleep unless he was next to me so of course I was up bright and early. Yes, we had phone sex but its nothing like the real thing; all it did was made me want him more. I went to get in the shower and saw Violet coming out.

"Girl, I miss my husband. I don't know about you but I'm ready to go and hop on my man's dick." She said and hi fived me on the way out. I loved Violet because she'd been through a lot with her husband too.

People can say what they want about us but when you love someone there will always be bumps and bruises along in your relationship. The perfect man or woman doesn't exist. We have to expect the unexpected and decide if it's worth staying or going. I have to say my man is worth staying and I wouldn't trade him in for anything.

"Get y'all ass up." I yelled at the three musketeers who were still asleep. Violet and I packed all our stuff up and took it down to the car.

"These bitches are strung the fuck out." Maria said coming out the shower.

"What are you talking about? Violet asked smiling.

"We know you two perverts are trying to rush home and fuck. Damn, I love my man too but y'all extra with the shit." I stuck my finger up at her and picked my phone up. I saw a message from James.

My husband: *I woke up and all I can think about is having you in my arms when you get here. I miss you baby and I'll see you soon.* A smile crept across my face and Iesha caught it.

"Damn. He must've said some good shit."

Me: *I can't wait to see you too. I can't text you too much this morning because they are already making fun of me.*

My husband: *What are they saying?"*

Me: *That we need to give each other a break and that Violet and I are strung out on you and Miguel.*

My husband: *LOL why did they say that?*

Me: *Because she and I been up and ready to go for over and hour.*

My husband: *I'll see you soon. Don't worry about them. You know they love the way we love.* I sent him back a smiling emoji and got in the car to leave.

We stopped at Perkins on the way to eat. It seemed like everyone was pre occupied on their phone like something was going on. When I asked they all said it was business but that shit was suspect. I ignored their ass the entire ride home. I was surprised to see we pulled up to James mother house but got out anyway. I stepped in the house and my daughters, Miguel's' mom *(Who is James aunt)*, my nieces, Violets daughter and my dad were in the house.

"Hey mommy." Patience said. She was starting to talk.

"Hey auntie." Summer came up and spoke.

"Now that my aunt is here can we get dressed now?" Lyric asked with her hand on her hip. Miguel's mom popped her in the mouth for getting smart. Her and Summer were a piece of work. I had to keep and eye on Patience around them.

230

"What is she talking about?" I asked James and Miguel's mom who were both hugging me at the same time.

"Baby, it's your wedding day." I felt the tears falling down my eyes unexpectedly. I knew James wanted to get married again but I didn't know it would be this soon. I was thinking next year. I started bombarding them with questions but they shut me down and made me go in the living room where the hair and makeup people were.

It took us almost four hours to get done and the wedding was in a half hour. We took tons of photos but no one was allowed to post any until after the wedding. James sent 2 Rolls Royce limos to pick us up. James and Miguel's mom took the kids in one while my dad and us drove in the other one.

I thought we were going to a church; imagine my surprise when we pulled up to my house. Cars were lined up and down the street and people were still coming. I didn't see too much security like I did at my sister's wedding. I just brushed it off because I knew nothing bad was going to happen. I watched all the kids walk down the aisle and then Maria and

Louis, Samantha and her husband, Violet and Miguel and then Iesha who was my Matron of Honor. Darius was in the front with James already.

"You ready?" My dad asked swooping his arm in mine.

"As ready as I'll ever be." I heard the song *Forever mine* by the O'Jays playing. I blew my breath and tried to stay calm. The door opened and once I laid eyes on my husband all I could do was cry. He stood there in all white looking handsome as ever. I was getting horny just staring at him. The pastor asked the congregation who was giving me away and my dad answered and gave my hand to James.

"Damn baby you are stunning. I can't wait to get you out of that later." He whispered in my ear as he lifted the veil.

"I can't wait either." I gave him a peck on his lips. The ceremony was beautiful and the vows James said had me crying hard. I could barely say mine but when I did he shed some tears as well. During the reception C.J. came up to us and handed me a present that he insisted I opened right away. It was a frame from things remembered with an ultrasound photo in it. James and I looked at each other confused.

"C.J. what is this?"

"My mom said to give this to you and that you would know what it meant." I could see how angry James got and put my hand on his lap.

"Thank you baby. Are you having fun?" I asked trying to lighten the mood.

"Yes. Can I make a toast?" I wasn't sure if that was the right thing to do now that he handed us this bullshit. James gave him a look that told him he better not say some dumb shit.

"Can we have everyone's attention? My nephew would like to give his first speech." Darius said.

"I want to say thank you for coming to my dad and stepmom's wedding." Everyone started clapping.

"Wait. I'm not done." The clapping stopped.

"Dad, I know we just met but I'm glad you are in my life. You are the best dad in the world." You could hear everyone say aww in the crowd.

"CiCi, you are the best stepmom even though my mom says bad things about you. I want to know if you can adopt me so I can live with you, my dad and my brothers and sisters forever." The room fell silent after he said that.

I saw the tears coming down his face and stood up. He dropped the microphone and ran over to hug me. Junior and Patience came over and hugged him too.

"I don't want to go home. Please let me stay with you." He was crying hysterically and hugging me tight, which caused me to cry.

"DJ play the music." Iesha yelled out. James walked over and took us all out and into the house. I didn't know what to say. I loved C.J. like he was my own son and for him to break down like that had my heart hurting. I was pacing back and forth in the living room.

"He's not going home." I said and James started smiling.

"What? Why are you smiling?" He lifted my chin up and kissed my lips.

"Because you love C.J. as if he were your own. Look at you protecting him and we don't even know if anything happened at his house."

"I don't care. If he doesn't want to go home he's not going. Call that bitch up and tell her she's signing over her rights to me."

"Damn baby. Calm down. You know that's going to be a fight."

"That's fine. I'll beat her ass and she won't have a choice." C.J. and Junior walked in the room.

"Let's go back to the reception and we'll deal with everything afterwards." James said taking my hand. After everyone left we all sat outside talking. C.J and Junior should've been asleep but they were out here trying to hang.

"Dad, if I have to go back there I'm going to run away." We were taking some trays in the house. He and I both stopped and turned around.

"Tell me why you don't want to go home." I bent down in front of him and waited for him to answer.

"You can't tell mommy I told you." James and I promised. Junior handed me C.J's phone and told me to go through the pictures. We got him a phone so him and Junior could talk whenever they wanted.

The pictures were of somebody's body with black and blue marks on them. They were on his legs and back. I dropped the phone and pulled C.J's shirt up and sure enough there were marks all over his back. We never noticed it because he knew how to bathe himself and didn't need help getting dressed.

"C.J. why was she doing this and why didn't you tell us?"

"She hates you CiCi. She does it every time I come home from over here."

"I'll be back. Junior get your aunt Iesha, Maria and Violet. Tell them I said come upstairs." He ran outside and did what I said.

"Where are you going?" James asked me helping me out of my gown.

"I'm about to go over her house and beat her ass."

"It's too late baby." He kissed my shoulders and started rubbing my breast from behind. Iesha knocked on the door and he told them to go away.

"What do you mean it's too late?"

"I had someone pick her up. She's on her way here." I was now face down on the bed with my ass in the air getting my pussy ate. He devoured me like I was his last meal before execution.

"Cum for me CiCi." The second he said that I gave him what he wanted. He entered me and fucked me so good I wanted to go to sleep. He made me throw some clothes on because Denise was probably here by now. On the way down the steps I heard screaming and both of us took off. C.J. was trying to get away from Denise and she must've yanked his arm too hard because it looked like it was dislocated.

"Ma, take him to the ER." He told his aunt to go with her.

"Junior go in your room and don't come out until I tell you too." He ran upstairs. I walked up to Denise and punched her so hard she was out for the count.

I continued beating on her until I felt James pull me off and tell me he had a surprise for me and I would need my energy for that. It didn't matter because Violet and Iesha jumped on her and by the time they finished, she looked dead.

Maria's crazy ass was drinking and laughing while Samantha shook her head. Say what you want but anyone who beats on a child like that, deserves exactly what she got if not more.

Two days went by since we beat the shit out of Denise. She was in the hospital and James had guards at her door. We were waiting for the lawyer to finish drawing up the adoption papers to have her sign them. I wanted him to make sure there was no way in hell she could get him back. It took another day for the papers to be drawn up and James took it up to the hospital. I told him it wasn't a good idea for me to do it because I would probably kill her. She gave him a sob story and didn't want to sign it but she really didn't have a choice.

Everything was documented as far as the photos, his arm was dislocated and we made sure he spoke with a child protective worker while he was in the hospital and we weren't present. She was able to speak with him and he told her everything which was good on our part because those people would've sent him right back to her.

"What's my surprise baby?" I asked while we laid in the bed. It had been two weeks since that shit happened. Our honeymoon was put on hold due to this surprise.

"Get dressed." It was after midnight and he was telling me to take a ride with him. It took us about forty-five minutes to get there and I saw Darius and Iesha pull up behind us with his mom and my dad.

"What is going on?" He took my hand and pulled me into him.

"You know I love you right. And there's nothing in this world I wouldn't do for you."

"I know baby. What's my surprise?" I was excited. When he opened the door my mouth hit the floor from the sight in front of me. The moment I've been waiting for was finally happening. I walked closer and pulled a chair to sit down and sat face to face with my mother Tasha Barnes.

Iesha

These past few years my sister and I have been through hell and back. I know I said it before but we continue to keep coming out on top. Yes, the niggas we married fucked up along the way but how many women can say they never went through shit and she still had his back or their man still had hers? Not many. Every setback only brought us back stronger and that's why at this very moment I love my man even more.

When Darius first woke me up and told me to get dressed I gave his ass a hard time. I had just gotten home from the restaurant and he had to have sex, which put me straight to sleep. I whined a little but still took the ride with him. I was surprised to see everyone there.

Cream was whispering sweet nothings in CiCi's ear as always and my dad had a look of evil on his face. I looked at Darius and he told me not to worry but there was a surprise on the other side of the door. CiCi walked in before I did and a few minutes later I heard screaming. I opened the door and the stench hit me first but the sight was worth it all.

There was my mother sitting in her own filth. There was a bucket, a chair and a rollout bed next to her. If you ask me she didn't need the bed, her ass could've slept on the floor for all I cared. She was going back and forth with CiCi about the four months she kept her hidden away. She had no remorse for what she did and said she would do it again. I didn't realize CiCi hit her until her head hit my foot. James and Darius sat in the back watching.

"And what the fuck do you want?" I kicked her in the mouth the minute she spoke. I guess it was a reflex. CiCi got up and went to sit with James so I took over the seat she was in.

"I just want to know why you hated me so much." When she was getting ready to answer the door opened and in walked James mom and my dad. She rubbed her eyes to make sure she wasn't seeing shit.

"I'm alive and well Tasha. No thanks to you."

"But how? I poisoned you?" My dad told her how Ms. Thomas came by and took him to a different doctor when she was on vacation and informed him that he didn't have cancer and was being poisoned. The funeral was staged and since white people looked the same it wasn't even his body.

The morgue had someone who resembled him and their mom paid a good amount of money to the other family to use the body at the funeral. The look on James and Darius face let us know they had no clue either. He told her how he moved down to Florida to get away and came back when the time was right but remained out of sight.

"Fuck you and that hoe. If it wasn't for her we would be together." My mother spat out blaming everything on him.

"And you. You're just a product of one of the many whores he fucked around with." At that moment it was as if my world came crashing down. I heard CiCi saying what the fuck and my dad telling my mother to shut the fuck up. Ms. Thomas touched my dad's arm and told him it's time to tell her.

"Tell me what dad?" Darius came over and traded spots with me and sat me on his lap. I looked at him but he shrugged his shoulders like he had no idea either.

"Yea tell her dad. Tell that dumb bitch the truth." CiCi hit her again this time knocking her out the chair.

"Iesha what I'm about to tell you is going to shock you. I kept you in the dark because I promised your mother I would never bring it up but it looks like I have no choice."

"Huh?" I was confused as hell.

"Iesha, Tasha is not your mother." He said and I felt my body get weak.

"Baby, are you ok?" I heard Darius talking and I tried to answer but the words wouldn't come out.

"Iesha, when Tasha gave birth to CiCi we were the happiest people on the planet. A few months later she and I decided to have another baby. Unfortunately, Tasha miscarried and hemorrhaged so bad she needed a full hysterectomy and could no longer birth any more kids. I was by her side and told her we could adopt but she wasn't hearing it. She fell into a state of depression, cut herself off from the world including me and CiCi. One day I was out with CiCi and bumped into your mom.

She and I became friends and when Tasha was out of it. One thing led to another and I found myself in bed with your mom. She and I continued the affair for a few months. Tasha

243

started coming back around and I cut her off but we stayed friends. One day out of the blue she called and said she was in labor. I wasn't sure why she called me but I went to the hospital to be there for her. Long story short she told me she was pregnant with my daughter and when you came out I knew you were mine. You and CiCi looked just alike."

"My daughter doesn't look like that bitch." Tasha said getting up off the floor.

"That explains why she hated me all this time. But why? I didn't have anything to do with what you and my mom did."

"So what? My husband wasn't supposed to have another child outside of our marriage. Now look both of you two idiots are dealing with the same shit with these assholes." I felt Darius try to get up and whispered not to in his ear.

"Where is my mother? Who is she? Why did you keep it from me this long?"

"Iesha, your mom passed away a hour after she had you. Her blood pressure was extremely high and she had a massive heart attack." I covered my mouth and let the tears fall.

"She said she fell in love again after seeing you."

"How could you keep this from me? All these years of her beating on me and treating me like shit?"

"I know Iesha and I'm sorry. Why do you think I made you stay up under me all the time? I was always there when the school called and I spoiled you. Your mom felt bad for having you with me knowing I was married and told me never to tell you about her. She asked me to take you and have Tasha claim you as her daughter. At first Tasha was good with you. I don't know what happened." He said pulling me up to hug him. I didn't want to forgive him after all I went through but I understood why he did it. I just wish I met my mother.

"Every time I looked in her face I saw your betrayal. That's why? Is that good enough for you? I'm over this father daughter shit. CiCi you want to know why I beat you like that? It was because I couldn't get to her and the fact that you let that nigga turn you against me. Before him you and I were close and nothing anyone did could change our relationship. Iesha kept getting in the way and yea you defended her too but you went to war with me over them."

"WHAT? You threw his son in my arms what did you think he would do? Then you tried to kill my sister and niece."

"That bitch isn't your sister."

"THAT IS MY FUCKING SISTER. YOU NOT BEING HER MOTHER DON'T MEAN SHIT. THAT'S MY SISTER AND YOU DAMN RIGHT I'M GOING TO WAR WITH YOU FOR HER, MY HUSBAND, MY DAD, MY KIDS AND ALL MY INLAWS, NIECES, NEPHEWS AND ANYONE ELSE I LOVE. WHAT YOU THOUGHT THIS WAS?" I never saw my sister that hype or even talk to her mother like that before.

"CICI you were never like this. Why did you turn on me?"

"You will not sit here and play victim. What you did to my sister can never be forgiven and I was going to do the honors of ending your life but I would much rather enjoy watching her doing it." CiCi handed me the gun and stepped away.

"What are you waiting for bitch? Just do it." I heard Tasha yell out but I couldn't do it. After everything she did to me I still loved her. She was the only mother I knew. I dropped the gun and fell into Darius arms. He picked me up and carried me out to the car. I heard a few shots on the way out but didn't even bother to look back. The shit was finally over.

****

My dad showed me where my mom was buried and we sat out there together with Darius, my kids, his mom, my sister and her family to clean off her tombstone and spend time with her.

I know people think its crazy but I felt a presence while I was standing there and I know it was her. I sat there and talked to her for a little while. Afterwards, I finally felt like I was at peace and could move on with my life without anyone out there trying to end mine.

The End....

CPSIA information can be obtained
at www.ICGtesting.com
Printed in the USA
LVHW041625130819
627493LV00003B/375/P